The WORLD'S GREATEST UNDERACHIEVER Takes on the UNIVERSE

The World's Greatest Underachiever series

*The World's Greatest Underachiever
Takes on the Universe*

(Bind-up of *The World's Greatest Underachiever and the Crazy Classroom Cascade*
and *The World's Greatest Underachiever and the Crunchy Pickle Disaster*)

*The World's Greatest Underachiever
and the Crazy Classroom Cascade*

*The World's Greatest Underachiever
and the Crunchy Pickle Disaster*

*The World's Greatest Underachiever
and the Lucky Monkey Socks*

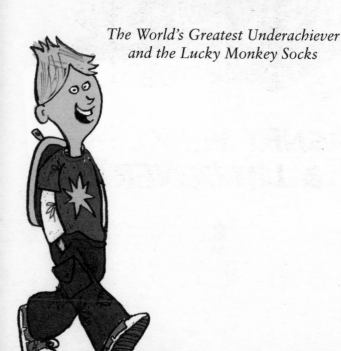

HANK ZIPZER

The WORLD'S GREATEST UNDERACHIEVER Takes on the UNIVERSE

HENRY WINKLER & LIN OLIVER

WALKER
BOOKS

First published individually in Great Britain as
Hank Zipzer the World's Greatest Underachiever: Niagara Falls – Or Does It? (2008)
and *Hank Zipzer the World's Greatest Underachiever: I Got a "D" in Salami* (2008)
by Walker Books Ltd, 87 Vauxhall Walk, London SE11 5HJ

First published in the United States as
Hank Zipzer #01: Niagara Falls – Or Does It? (2003)
and *Hank Zipzer #02: I Got a "D" in Salami* (2003) by Henry Winkler and Lin Oliver.
Published by arrangement with Grosset & Dunlap™, a division of Penguin Young
Readers Group, a member of Penguin Group (USA) Inc. All rights reserved.

This bind-up edition published 2011

2 4 6 8 10 9 7 5 3 1

Text © 2003, 2011 Henry Winkler and Lin Oliver Productions, Inc.
Cover illustration, design and interior illustrations © 2011 Nigel Baines

This book has been typeset in Sabon

Printed and bound in Great Britain by Clays Ltd, St Ives plc

British Library Cataloguing in Publication Data:
a catalogue record for this book is available from the British Library

ISBN 978-1-4063-4027-3

www.walker.co.uk

HANK ZIPZER

and the CRAZY CLASSROOM CASCADE

HANK ZIPZER

and the CRUNCHY PICKLE DISASTER

I dedicate this book to my wife Stacey and my three children, Jed, Zoe and Max, because it's their love that gave me the strength to do this in the first place – H.W.

This book is for my four fabulous men – Alan, Theo, Oliver and Cole. With love and potato leek soup – L.O.

HANK ZIPZER

The WORLD'S GREATEST UNDERACHIEVER

and the CRAZY CLASSROOM CASCADE

CHAPTER 1

It started to buzz. I looked up. The loudspeaker above the door crackled and buzzed again. Then it started to shake. It was coming alive!

"Hank Zipzer!" the loudspeaker said. "Report to Mr Love's office at once."

I put my hands over my ears and slid down in my chair.

How did it know my name? It was only the first hour of the first day of school, and already my name was coming out of that box on the wall.

Everyone in class stared at me. Some kids giggled. A few of them whispered. But not Nick McKelty. Nope – he cupped his hands over his big mouth and shouted, "Way to go, Zipper Boy!"

My teacher, Ms Adolf, shot me a really nasty look.

Show no fear, I thought. *Walk the walk.*

I stood up and strutted to the door like Shaquille O'Neal taking centre court. OK, so I wear a size-four shoe and he wears a size twenty-three – it's the attitude that matters. I'm big on attitude. Small on shoe but big on attitude.

When I reached the door, I turned to my best friend, Frankie Townsend. "If I don't come back," I told him, "you can have my protractor."

"Don't forget to breathe in there," Frankie whispered. "Remember, Zip, oxygen is power."

Frankie is very big on oxygen. Whenever I'm nervous, he always tells me to take some deep breaths. He learned that from his mum, who is a yoga teacher. She's really good at yoga. In fact, she's not good, she's great. She is so flexible, she can lift up her leg and put her foot in her pocket!

Even though I was going to the head teacher's office, I was determined to leave with style, my head held high. I flashed the class my best smile, the one where I show both my top and bottom teeth. Then, in the middle of maybe the greatest exit ever, the loudspeaker buzzed again.

"And don't you dare stop in the toilets, young man," it said.

Now how did it know I was going to do that?

Everyone laughed as I left.

"No laughing in class!" Ms Adolf shouted, banging on her desk with this pointer stick she has.

That's one of her rules. Ms Adolf doesn't believe in laughing. She thinks fourth-graders laugh way too much.

There are two fourth-grade teachers in my school. One is named Mr Sicilian, and he's really nice. He plays football with everyone at break time and never gives homework at the weekend. The other is Ms Adolf. She doesn't play any games and gives two tons of homework even on weekends. My luck, I got Ms Adolf.

I could practically hear my heart pounding as I walked down the corridor. Mr Love has a way of making you nervous, especially when you don't know what you've done wrong.

I was trying not to think about him, so I looked at all the "Welcome Back" decorations in the corridor instead. The corridors at my school are painted yuck green. You know, the colour of melted pistachio ice cream. But the decorations really helped to cheer things up. I liked Miss Hart's door, which had an underwater theme. All the fifth-graders in her class had pasted pictures of their faces on to octopus heads. Mr Sicilian's was my favourite. All the kids' heads were footballs. I told you he was cool.

When I reached the stairs, I thought about sliding down the banister, but I was already in enough trouble, so I took the stairs – two at a time. My mouth was dry when I got to the bottom, so I stopped at the water fountain to have a drink.

Just as I took the first gulp, the loudspeaker buzzed again.

"I'm waiting, Mr Zipzer," it said. Mr Love has the kind of voice that sounds like it belongs to a really tall man with a lot of bushy, black hair. But actually, Mr Love is short and bald except for a little fringe of red hair.

I ran down the corridor. I couldn't get into trouble for running in the corridors if the place I was running to was the head teacher's office, right?

When I got to the office, I took a deep breath. I looked up at the sign above the door. LELAND LOVE, HEAD TEACHER, it said. I had been here before. Many times. Too many times. Way, way, way too many times.

Slowly, I pushed open the door. I walked inside and came face to face with the five of them. No, not people – there was only one person there. I'm talking about *things*. The things on Mr Love's face: two eyes, two ears and one mole on his cheek that looked like the Statue of Liberty without the torch. I don't know if it's possible for a mole to frown, but trust me, this one did not look happy.

"Approach me, young man," Head Teacher Love said.

I wanted to, I really did, but my feet were stuck on his carpet. It was as if I had big wads of chewing gum stuck to the soles of my shoes.

"Were you or were you not late today?" Head Teacher Love asked.

I didn't answer because I've found that when Leland Love asks a question, he likes to answer it himself.

"You were seventeen minutes late," he said.

See what I mean?

"Did we not have this talk thirty times in third grade, fifteen times in second grade, and I won't even refer to first grade?" Mr Love's face twitched. It looked like the Statue of Liberty was doing a hula dance.

I tried not to laugh. That would have got me into even bigger trouble.

"We've had this talk many times," he answered himself. See, he did it again.

I looked down at my feet, mostly to stop myself from staring at the Statue of Liberty mole. Once you focus on that thing, it's really hard to take your eyes off it. I noticed that I had put on odd socks again. One had a Nike swoosh and the other was just your basic Walmart sock.

"If there's one thing I want you to learn from your experience at PS 87, it is this—" Mr Love was using his bushy-hair-tall-man voice. "Are you listening, young man?"

"I've got both ears working, sir."

Actually, I *was* listening. I really was curious to hear the single most important thing I was supposed to learn in my whole entire primary school career.

Head Teacher Love cleared his throat. "Always be on time, when time is involved," he said.

Wow. There it was. Now, if I could just figure out what it meant.

"Explain to me how it is possible that you were late on the very first day of school," he said.

OK, I'll be honest with you. I am late a lot, but I don't mean to be. In fact, I try really hard to have everything ready on time – my pencils all sharpened; my three ballpoint pens ready to roll; a protractor, a ruler *and* a compass in my pencil case. But this morning I had a problem. I'm pretty sure

I remember putting my rucksack on my desk chair before I went to bed. But somehow, and I don't have an exact reason for this, my rucksack played hide-and-seek during the night and this morning it took me twenty minutes to find it. It was in the cupboard by the front door. But try telling that to Leland Love.

"I'm waiting for an answer," said Head Teacher Love.

And all that squeaked out of me was, "Can't explain it, sir."

"Well then, absorb this," he said, "because I'm only going to say it once. Punctuality and the fourth grade go hand in hand." He paused, then said it again, just like I knew he would. "Punctuality and the fourth grade go hand in hand."

I'm not sure but I think the Statue of Liberty on his face nodded in agreement.

CHAPTER 2

I can't believe I'm saying this, but it was actually a relief to get back to Ms Adolf's class … for about twenty seconds, anyway.

As soon as I slid into my chair, the words "Five full paragraphs are required" came flying out of Ms Adolf's mouth like heat-seeking missiles.

I looked around. All the other kids were writing in their homework books. I reached for my homework book too, but it was missing in action. I thought maybe I had left it in the middle drawer of my desk at home, underneath my broken watch collection. Or maybe on the kitchen table.

"The topic for your essay is: what I did in the summer holidays," Ms Adolf went on. As she wrote the words on the blackboard, I noticed that her skirt had lots of chalk marks in the butt region. That happens to teachers when they lean against the blackboard, but I had never seen chalk marks like this before. They looked like donkey ears. When I thought of Ms Adolf with a donkey on her bum, I couldn't help myself. I laughed out loud.

"Henry, I see nothing funny," Ms Adolf said. Of course she didn't. That's because she couldn't see her rear end.

I bit my lip and tried to concentrate.

"I expect you to write an opening paragraph, a concluding paragraph and three supporting paragraphs," Ms Adolf was saying.

I raised my hand.

"Exactly how long does a paragraph have to be?" I asked.

Everyone laughed, which was strange, because I wasn't trying to be funny. Ms Adolf didn't laugh. She got little red splotches on her neck, like the kind my sister, Emily, gets when she's really mad.

"Well, Henry," Ms Adolf said, saying my name

as if it smelled bad. "We will all learn that from you, since you'll be the first one to read your essay out loud to the class."

Ms Adolf walked to her desk. She wore a cord round her neck with a small key on it. The key was silver and so shiny that she must have polished it every night. She slipped the cord off and unlocked the top drawer of her desk with the key. I wondered what could be in there that had to be locked up. I looked at Frankie, who knew what I was thinking.

"Maybe she's got a big wad of cash in there," he whispered.

"Or jewels," said our friend Ashley Wong, who loves jewellery.

But when Ms Adolf opened the drawer, the only thing she took out was her register. She picked it up and started to write.

"Henry Zipzer, Monday at nine-fifteen," she said. "We will all look forward to hearing your essay then. Is that clear, Henry?"

"Ms Adolf," I said, "do you think you could call me Hank?"

"Why would I call you *Hank* when *Henry* is a perfectly fine name?" she said. She locked up her register and slipped the key back over her head.

"It's what my friends call me."

"Well, *I* am not your friend," Ms Adolf said. As if I hadn't already figured that out.

She reached down and picked a tiny piece of fluff off her skirt. I mean, it was so tiny you needed a microscope to see it. She held the bit of fluff in her hand and walked it carefully over to the bin. When she dropped it in, I'm telling you, I saw nothing leave her fingers.

I wondered why Ms Adolf would care so much about a piece of fluff. It's not like she looks that good anyway. All she ever wears are a grey skirt and a grey blouse, which match her grey hair and grey glasses, not to mention her grey face.

"Remember, class, that's *five* paragraphs," she said. "And neatness counts. I'll be expecting your very best work. That includes you, Henry."

Smile, Hank, I thought. *Nod your head, up and down. You can do this. Five paragraphs. What's the big deal? You've got six days.*

Oh come on, who am I kidding? I can't

even write *one* good sentence. So how am I ever going to write an entire five-paragraph essay? Ms Adolf might as well have asked me to ski down Mount Everest ... backwards ... blindfolded ... and butt naked.

CHAPTER 3

At lunch, I sat at the table and stared at my vegetarian bologna-sausage sandwich. Most of the other kids were waiting in the hot food queue. It was either macaroni cheese day or tuna-melt day. Or maybe it was both. I couldn't tell without looking at the menu, because all school food smells the same.

I looked around the dining room and spotted Frankie. He had just bought some milk and was laughing and talking with Katie Sperling and Kim Paulson, only the two most beautiful girls in the entire school. When Frankie smiles, he gets this huge dimple in his cheek. As he walked, he kept flashing the girls The Big Dimple. And, man, was it working! They were following him to our table. I couldn't believe it – Katie Sperling and Kim Paulson were going to sit down with us! That is, until Robert Upchurch cut in front of them and took the seat opposite me.

"Hey, Hank, mind if I sit here?" he asked.

"Yes," I answered, but it was too late.

When Katie and Kim saw Robert, they swerved left – at least I think it was left. Maybe it was right. It's hard for me to keep track of directions. Anyway, they went down a totally different aisle and sat with Ryan Shimozato and his friends. Robert isn't exactly a girl magnet. He has a neck the size of a pencil and always wears a starchy white shirt with a tie. (That's right, I said a *tie*.) Add to that the fact that he's the most boring person on the planet and you can't blame the girls for picking another table.

Frankie flopped down next to me. "Thanks, Robert," he said. "Nice work."

"What'd I do?" Robert asked. Poor kid, he really didn't have a clue.

Robert has just started third grade. Since the third-graders and fourth-graders at my school eat lunch together, this was the first day he'd had a chance to sit with us. We don't really want him hanging around with us, but he lives in the same block of flats as Frankie, Ashley and me, so he thinks he has the right to tag along everywhere.

Frankie glanced at my sandwich and made a face. He's been making faces at my lunches ever since we were in preschool.

"I see your mum's at it again," he said. "What's she calling this, soy surprise?"

"It's bologna," I told him.

"Bologna and I go *way* back," said Frankie, "and this is no bologna!"

I don't know if you've had vegetarian bologna before, but I don't think you've ever had my *mum's* vegetarian bologna. She thinks she invented it, which proves she should keep her thoughts to herself. My mum's vegetarian bologna tastes like nothing you've ever put in your mouth. Let's just say it's round, ground, pinkish leaves of grass. Let's just say it's non-food.

Ever since my mother took over Papa Pete's deli, she has been experimenting like crazy with food. Unfortunately for me, my lunch is her laboratory. Vegetarian bologna is only one of her experiments. You haven't lived until you've tried her soy salami. Papa Pete says it's a crime what she does to salami.

By the way, Papa Pete is my grandpa. He's the best. Sometimes I get the feeling that he's the only person who understands me. He never ever thinks I'm stupid or lazy.

"Actually, bologna is a very interesting word,"

Robert said through a mouthful of macaroni cheese.

Frankie and I looked at each other. You know how when you have a best friend, you and the other person often think the same thing at the same time? We were both thinking, *Somebody get me out of this conversation!*

"What's especially interesting is that bologna contains a silent *g*, just like the silent *k* in *knock* or *knight*," Robert went on.

Robert knows everything. That's why he skipped second grade. I think it's great to know a lot of things. I just don't think you have to say them all the time. Like Robert will name all the James Bond movies in order, including the year they came out, even when no one asks him. And don't even start him on world capitals. He'll tell you the capital of Indonesia right in the middle of a dodgeball game. The other day he just looked at me and said, "The human body has enough iron to make one nail." He said it like it was a totally normal thing to say!

"Robert," I said, "why don't you go and sit with the third-graders."

"They're not interested in what I have to say," he said.

"We're not interested either," I said.

"Why not?" he answered. "Spelling is a very challenging subject."

"Challenging?" I said. "That's the understatement of the century. I can't spell to save my life. And it really bothers me too."

"I can't imagine not being able to spell," Robert said. "Doesn't it make you feel stupid?"

"Robert, will you give Zip a break?" said Frankie, giving him a noogie on the head. "Can't you see he's a troubled man?"

"What's wrong with you?" Robert asked.

"Ms Adolf is making us write an entire five-paragraph essay," I answered. "Neatness counts. Punctuation counts. Everything counts. Do you realize how impossible that is?"

Just then, Ashley slid on to the bench next to me and put her tray down. She had chosen both the macaroni cheese and the tuna-melt. Ashley likes variety – in everything. You should see her clothes. She covers them all with rhinestones – even her trainers. She's got one pair with a family of dolphins swimming in the ocean, in blue and green rhinestones. She glues them all on herself.

"What's impossible?" asked Ashley.

"Spelling," I said.

"Spelling is hard," she agreed.

"But this is impossible."

She picked up a cherry that was sitting on top of her fruit salad. She popped it into her mouth and ate it. Then her face got all twisted up and busy, like a chipmunk shelling an acorn. In no time, she stuck out her tongue and there was the cherry stem, tied in a perfect knot. Is Ashley Wong an amazing girl or what?

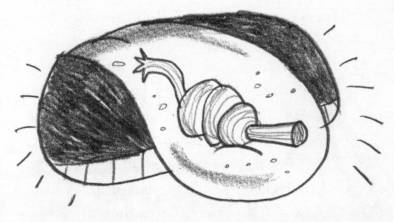

"Ashweena, that is so cool," said Frankie. Frankie has a nickname for everyone. He even calls my dad Mr Z. No one else I know even *talks* to my father.

"Does nobody care about my problem?" I said. "Is anybody listening?"

My friends stopped eating and looked at me.

"How am I going to write five perfect paragraphs by next Monday when I can't get what I'm thinking about down on paper?" I said. "My handwriting looks like a chicken stepped in tar and ran across the page."

"If a chicken stepped in tar, it would get stuck and couldn't run anywhere," Robert pointed out.

"Shut up, Robert," we all said together.

"I put commas in the wrong places," I continued. "My capital letters look weird. My lowercase letters look even weirder. My spelling – well, we all know about my spelling."

"Take a breath, Zip," said Frankie. "We'll figure it out. Hey, make friends with the dictionary. Let your fingers do the walking, if you know what I'm talking about."

Frankie is really good at school. He thinks maths is easy *and* get this – he reads for fun. I wish I could do that. I wish it was easier for me to read a book.

"You sound just like my father," I said. "He's always telling me to look up words in the dictionary."

Suddenly, Frankie grabbed his chest and fell to the ground, flopping around like he was some kind of alien. He's cool enough to be able to do a thing like that in the dining room. Even Katie Sperling and Kim Paulson were laughing. Not at him, either, but with him.

"That hurts!" he screamed. "Comparing me to Silent Stan, the crossword-puzzle man." (That's another one of Frankie's nicknames for my dad.)

31

Frankie got up and sat back down at the table. "Someone, please. What's a four-letter word for a root vegetable?" he said, doing a perfect imitation of my father working on a crossword puzzle.

We all cracked up. Milk came shooting out of Ashley's nose. It splattered all over her T-shirt, spraying the rhinestone self-portrait she had done. Drops of milk hung off the purple stones she had used for the frames of her glasses.

"Does anyone have a napkin?" she asked.

"Here, take mine," I told her. "My sandwich is never going to make it to my mouth anyway."

"Do me a favour, Zip," Frankie said. "Don't ever tell me that I sound like your father again."

"Then don't bring up the dictionary again," I said. "It's such a useless invention. At least for me."

"Don't tell that to Ms Adolf," said Ashley. "She's in love with dictionaries."

"They don't make any sense," I said. "I can't spell words because I can't sound them out. So how am I going to find them in a dictionary if I can't spell them in the first place? Do you know my dictionary has one thousand two hundred and fifty-six pages? Words get lost in there."

"Zip, you're forgetting to…"

"… breathe. I know, Frankie. I *am* breathing."

Frankie put his hand on my shoulder. "Look, it's just an essay, my man."

"Maybe for you," I said. "For me, it's torture."

Frankie reached into his lunchbox and pulled out a packet of Ding Dongs. He took one for himself and gave one to me.

"Listen up, Zip," he said. "We're supposed to write about what we did in our summer holidays, right? So just write about what happened to you. You had an awesome summer holiday – going to Canada and to Niagara Falls and getting to steer the boat all by yourself when the captain fell overboard. Man, that's cool stuff."

Ashley nearly choked on her second cherry stem.

"That's not what you told *me*," she said. "You told me your sister got seasick and threw up all over your plastic raincoat."

OK, OK, so sometimes I tell stories. But

they're not lies or anything. It's just that I think the world needs to be entertained. I happen to be good at it. Like Papa Pete says, "If you got it, flaunt it." Flaunt. There's another word I can't spell.

Suddenly, out of nowhere came a hand bigger than an average hand. Bigger than a tabletop. Then a head the size of Rhode Island appeared. Next came the smell of bad, bad breath – the kind that makes the gel in your hair lose its grip.

"That Ding Dong is mine," Nick McKelty said as he smashed what was once my chocolate bar into his oversized mouth. "I wuffofv deese."

Robert dived for cover under the table. Ashley shot milk again.

"Be my guest," I said. It was either that or have Nick the Tick pound my skull with his knuckles. Nick thinks that because he is the biggest guy in the fourth grade, everybody's lunch is his personal meal. We are his menu and he just takes whatever he wants.

Nick was looking for his second course. My instincts told me he was headed for Ashley's tuna-melt.

"Nick!" I said, yelling to catch his attention. "You don't want to eat that."

"Like you're going to stop me," he said, flashing me his stupid grin. The Ding Dong chocolate was wedged in the gap between his teeth so it looked like he had three front teeth.

"Did you hear about the tuna they just caught off Cape Cod that ate a licence plate from a car from Ohio?" I said to him, thinking fast. "There was so much metal ground up inside him that by the time he got to the shop he didn't need a tin."

I pointed to Ashley's sandwich. "That's him in there."

You could almost hear the small wheels grinding inside his huge blond head.

"I didn't want that pathetic sandwich anyway," he said. "I've got to save my appetite for the Knicks' basketball game tonight. My dad's got tickets for right next to the players' bench."

Nick's father owns the local bowling alley, McKelty's Roll 'N Bowl. Maybe that's why Nick the Tick thinks he has the right to act like a big shot all the time. All he does is brag, and none of it is ever true.

OK, like I said before, I tell stories sometimes too. But let's get one thing straight: my stories are purely for entertainment purposes. Nick's stories are to make him seem cool. Which he's not, I might add. Like, he says his father has the best seats for every sporting event in the United States of America. The truth is, they mostly watch the games on the TV at the bowling alley. That's what we call The McKelty Factor. Truth times a hundred.

In any case, Nick walked away. Ashley smiled at me. "Thanks, Hank," she said.

I felt proud. I had saved her lunch.

"You are amazing, Zip," Frankie said. "You have so much trouble with so many things, but never with your mouth. It's a brilliant mouth."

I thought about that. If my brilliant mouth worked on Nick McKelty, why couldn't it work on Ms Adolf?

I took out a piece of paper and a pencil. I had a plan.

CHAPTER 4

Before lunch ended, I decided to find Ms Adolf and have a little chat. She was sitting at her desk, finishing her lunch. Two big napkins covered most of her. Just her shoes were showing. They were grey. She was eating a banana that was so brown you couldn't even tell it had ever been yellow.

"May I talk to you for a minute, Ms Adolf?" I asked from the doorway.

She waved me inside.

"I've been thinking a lot about my essay," I began.

"I'm glad to hear that, Henry," she said.

37

"What I've been thinking about, exactly, is that it would really benefit you if I don't write this essay."

"Is that so?" she said. She tossed the banana skin into the bin.

"In fact, I've spent a good part of my lunch break writing a list of ten really excellent reasons why I shouldn't write this essay."

I pulled the piece of paper from my back pocket and flattened it out on her desk with the palm of my hand. There was a big, greasy smudge on it. And it really, really smelled like tuna fish. I have to admit it was pretty disgusting.

"Sorry," I said, trying to rub it off. "It was tuna-melt day. Just pretend it's a scratch-and-sniff."

I smiled. Ms Adolf didn't.

That wasn't a good start, but I had to think positively. I stood very quietly while she read the list.

TEN REASONS WHY HANK ZIPZER SHOULD NOT WRITE A FIVE-PARAGRAPH ESSAY ON "WHAT I DID THIS SUMMER"

1. Every pen I own runs out of ink.
2. My thoughts are controlled by alien beings who make me write in a strange language.
3. We couldn't go anywhere over the summer because my dog had a nervous breakdown.
4. I'm highly allergic to lined paper.
5. When I write, my fingers stick together.
6. If I sit too long, my bum falls asleep and snores, which keeps my sister awake.
7. Every time I write an essay, my dog Cheerio eats it for breakfast before I can get to school. So why try?
8. My computer keyboard is missing eleven letters — v, c, t, s, m and all the vowels including y and w.
9.
10.

The last two reasons were on the tip of my tongue, but I just couldn't get them to the tip of my pencil.

Ms Adolf put down the list and looked up at me. "This is very creative," she said.

Creative. Creative is good. My plan was working.

"I hope you'll use some of this creativity in your essay," she went on. "I look forward to hearing you read your written words on Monday morning."

Then she took my list, crumpled it up and tossed it in the bin. *There is my creativity,* I thought – *stuck to the top of a brown banana skin.*

CHAPTER 5

Three, two, one. Brrriinnngg. The bell. After an endless afternoon of alphabetizing practice, the first day of fourth grade was finally over. Frankie and I looked at each other. We were free men.

Frankie, Ashley and I ran downstairs and practically flew out the front door of the school building. Papa Pete was waiting outside to walk us home. He was helping Mr Baker, the lollipop man, take the little kids across the road. Papa Pete is my mother's father. He also happens to be one of the greatest human beings on the face of the earth.

"There he is," said Frankie, waving to Papa

Pete. "Get your cheeks ready."

When Papa Pete sees you, he gives you a big pinch and says, "I love this cheek and everything that's attached to it." I know this sounds like it's annoying, but actually it makes you feel really good.

Papa Pete gave us each a pinch and a hug. "I hardly recognized you kids," he said. "You look so much older now that you're in the fourth grade."

We had hoped that this would be the year we'd be allowed to walk home from school by ourselves. After all, Frankie, Ashley and I lived in the same block of flats, so we could all walk together. Safety in numbers, we all told our parents. But we were all turned down flat. New York City is not a place for kids to be wandering around alone, our parents said.

OK, we could live with that, because having Papa Pete walk you home is actually pretty fun. He walks a few metres behind us to make it *look* like we're walking alone. Papa Pete is so big that there is no way we could lose him in a crowd, even if we tried. It's not that he's tall, he's just large, the way a grizzly bear is large. My Grandma Jennie used to call him her big, cuddly grizzly bear. Maybe that was because he also has a ton of curly black hair on his arms and a huge moustache he calls his handlebars. After he eats something messy, he'll always say, "Tell me, Hank. Do I have anything hanging off the old handlebars?" I always tell him if he does, because he doesn't want to be embarrassed.

We headed up Amsterdam Avenue. We walked a couple of blocks and passed Harvey's, our favourite pizza place. It's no wider than a corridor, but they have the greatest Cherry Cokes and pizza there. You can smell it blocks away.

"I say we stop in for a slice," Frankie said.

Papa Pete shook his head. "Hold on, partner. We've got bigger bread to butter."

When Papa Pete says a thing like that, you don't argue. He's always got something great waiting for you.

We passed the man on the corner selling sunglasses. "Hey, gentlemen and lady," he said to us. "I've got a special pair just for your face."

Ashley stopped to look at a pair of rhinestone-covered glasses, but Frankie and I pulled her away. You can't let Ashley get started on rhinestones or you'll be there all day. She's a complete rhinestone nut.

Messengers on motorbikes whizzed by us. Mums coming back from the park pushed their babies in buggies. I love to see the babies' feet hanging out of the buggies. It always amazes me that inside their little bitty feet are big feet waiting to pop out and play baseball.

A couple of blocks up, we passed my mum's deli, the one Papa Pete started. It's called The Crunchy Pickle. They serve sandwiches so high they have to be held together with a toothpick. I waved at Carlos, who works behind the counter. I could see him shouting something, and even though I couldn't hear him, I knew he was saying, "Hey, Little Man."

"Hey, Big Man," I called back.

When we got to our block of flats, Frankie and Ashley started to go inside. Papa Pete steered them back on to the pavement.

"You haven't forgotten, have you?" he said.

"We have some business to conduct. I was thinking maybe you could come to my office."

Papa Pete's "office" is McKelty's Roll 'N Bowl. It's his hangout, his home from home. Everyone there knows him. He's the best senior bowler on the Upper West Side of Manhattan.

"I'll have to ask my parents," Ashley said.

"I took the liberty of phoning the good Doctors Wong," said Papa Pete, "and they said you don't have to be home until six." Although Ashley's parents are both doctors, Papa Pete is the only one I know who calls them "the good Doctors Wong". They don't seem to mind, though.

"I don't think my mum will let me go," Frankie said. "My dad teaches tonight and she likes me home."

Frankie's dad teaches African-American studies at Columbia University, which is thirty-eight blocks uptown. Once, his dad let me go to one of his lectures. He talked for almost two hours. I don't think I'll ever go to university if you have to sit still and listen to someone talk for two hours – and take notes at the same time.

"Fortunately for you, your mother was standing

on her head when I called," Papa Pete said to Frankie, "so I spoke to your father. When I explained that we were discussing important business, he said OK."

That was all we needed to hear. We took off for McKelty's, which is only a couple of blocks from our building. It's located on the second floor above the ninety-nine-cent shop, where I do most of my present buying. I bought my mum some earrings there for Mother's Day. She doesn't wear them much, though, because they hurt her lobes. Lots of people who shop at the ninety-nine-cent shop don't even realize that there's a bowling alley upstairs. You can hardly see it from the street, but it's got fifteen lanes, video games and a coffee shop, too.

When we got to McKelty's, the lanes were full of Papa Pete's friends. They were all wearing their different coloured team shirts. They waved at us as we took a seat in one of the red plastic booths in the coffee shop.

"Fern!" Papa Pete called out. "Three root-beer floats for my grandkids here."

The fact that Frankie is African-American and Ashley's parents are from Taiwan doesn't stop Papa Pete from calling them his grandkids. That's another thing I love about him. And another is that he'll always buy you as many root beer floats as you want without ever mentioning that they will spoil your appetite for dinner.

Fern, who has been working at McKelty's for like a hundred and fifty years, brought us our root-beer floats.

As we were slurping down the last of our ice cream, Papa Pete started talking. "OK, let's get down to business," he said, wiping some whipped cream from his moustache. "I believe you've got a little something to show me."

I haven't mentioned this before, because sometimes I forget things, but Frankie is an outrageous magician. He doesn't just do the tricks you can buy in the shops, either. He makes up his own. Anybody can make a nickel disappear and then pull it out of your ear. But Frankie can make a *quarter* disappear and then have five nickels drop out of his nose. Now *that's* what I call *magic*.

Papa Pete was thinking of hiring him to be the entertainment at his Bowling League's Start of the Season Party. His team is called The Chopped

Livers. Everything about Papa Pete has to do with the deli he used to own – like his two parakeets are named Lox and Bagels. I'm surprised he didn't name my mother Pickled Herring.

"Let's see what you can do," Papa Pete said to Frankie.

"You mean you're making the kid audition?" Fern said.

"Business is business," answered Papa Pete, winking at Ashley and pinching my cheek, all at the same time.

Frankie reached into his rucksack, got out three red cups and placed them in a row on the table.

"What you see before you are three ordinary red cups," he began. He took out two small- and one medium-sized royal blue sponge balls that he mushed together into the palm of his hand. He asked Ashley to blow on his closed hand three times, then opened his palm and the balls had transformed into one big blue sponge ball. He put that ball under the middle red cup. He moved all the cups around in a flurry, then put them in a stack.

"*Zengawii!*" chanted Frankie. It's a word he made up when he went to Zimbabwe with his parents a couple of years ago. Frankie says it has magical powers.

He lifted the stack of cups high in the air. There on the table were two small- and one medium-sized sponge balls.

ZENGAWII!

"You're hired," Papa Pete said, applauding. "Do you want the job?"

"Could I have a word with my associates for a moment?" I asked Papa Pete. "In private."

I pulled Frankie and Ashley off to the side.

"I see a future here for us all," I said. "Frankie, you're the head magician, but you're going to need an assistant, which is me. And we'll need a business manager. That's you, Ashley. You'll make us millionaires."

"I want to be an assistant, too," Ashley said.

"OK," I said. "We'll take turns. But you still have to be the money person, because I'm dangerous with numbers." Last week, I went to buy a slice of pizza and they were out of dollar bills, so the guy gave me change all in coins. I just had to trust that he had given me the right change, because there was no way I could add it all up in my head. I would have needed a pad of paper, a pencil and my sister, Emily, who is like a human calculator, to figure it out.

"OK," said Ashley. "Since I'm the business person, let me do the talking."

"Go for it, Ashweena," said Frankie, slapping her a high five.

We went back over to Papa Pete.

"In the last few minutes, we've formed a partnership," said Ashley. "We've considered your offer, and my partners and I believe that for seventy-five dollars, we can put on a magic show that will never be forgotten."

"I believe," said Papa Pete, tugging on his moustache, "that for *thirty* dollars, you can put on a magic show that I'll like even better."

"Take it," I whispered in Ashley's ear. "It'll only go down from here."

"Deal," Ashley said. And she stuck out her hand.

Papa Pete shook it and said, "And of course, for this kind of money, I'd hope to see a small live furry thing coming out of a top hat. I always enjoy that."

"No problem," Ashley said.

Frankie and I shot each other panicked looks. Why was she promising that? We didn't have a small live furry thing.

We grabbed Ashley by the arm and pulled her over to the video game room. I knew I had to get her away from Papa Pete before she agreed to make the Empire State Building disappear.

"What were you thinking?" I said to Ashley.

"I was thinking about a rabbit," she said. "It's

always nice to pull a rabbit out of a hat."

"Earth to Ashley," said Frankie. "We don't have a rabbit."

"That's a good point," she said.

"Now what are we going to do?" I asked. "You promised Papa Pete we'd pull a live furry thing out of a top hat! He's counting on it."

Ashley just smiled. "You'll think of something, Hank. You always do."

CHAPTER 6

On the walk home, we couldn't stop coming up with names for our new magic business. When we left McKelty's, we thought The Magic Trio sounded really good. Smooth and simple. By the time we crossed the road, we had switched to something flashier, like The Three Magicteers. When we saw a neon sign in front of the all-night laundrette, we came up with Magic: Open All Night. By 83rd Street, Frankie was convinced we should be The Mystical Magical Dudes. By 82nd Street, Ashley was pushing for The Disappearing Act.

By the time we reached 78th street, we had decided. We were Magik 3. Frankie thought we should definitely spell Magic with a *k* because it looks cool. That was fine with me, since that's the way I thought it was spelled anyway.

It felt so great to have a name. And a plan. We figured we'd start our career at McKelty's Roll 'N Bowl. Then we'd move on to kids' parties and become known all over the entire West Side. Next, we'd take our show downtown. And finally on to Madison Square Garden where there'd be thousands of fans, chanting our name: "Magik 3! Magik 3! Magik 3!"

We decided to start rehearsals right away, so we scheduled a kick-off meeting for right after dinner. I was so excited about Magik 3 that I couldn't wait to go upstairs and tell my parents about us. I buzzed our flat number. My sister, Emily, answered the intercom.

"Who's there?" she asked.

"Open sesame," I said in my magician assistant's voice.

"Hank? Is that you? Why do you sound so weird?"

"The Mighty Zengawii requests that you let him in ... in ... in..." I gave my voice this really cool echo. Frankie and Ashley cracked up.

"Mum!" Emily yelled. "Hank's downstairs and he thinks he's being funny but he's not."

"Just buzz him in, honey," I heard my mum say over the sound of the blender in the kitchen.

"I'm letting you in," Emily said. "But if it were up to me, I'd leave you standing down there until you acted normal."

That's a strange thing to say coming from Emily, who's about as *un*normal as a person can be.

Frankie, Ashley and I got into the lift and pressed for our floors. I live on ten, which is the top floor. Frankie lives on six and Ashley lives on four. As we rode up, I imagined the three of us dressed in black capes and top hats. We'd all have moustaches. Ashley would look so funny in a moustache. The lift stopped at her floor. I pushed the door open and held it with my foot. We all put our hands out and placed them on top of one another's.

"Magik 3 rules," we chanted.

Ashley got out. Frankie and I headed for six.

"Watch this," said Frankie. He snapped his fingers and said, "Zengawii." The lift stopped and the door opened on his floor.

I rode by myself up to ten. When I got out, I shoved my key into the lock and made my entrance into the flat.

"Good evening, ladies and gentlemen of the Zipzer family," I said, with a sweep of my imaginary cape. "Welcome to the most astounding show you will ever behold, featuring the amazing talents of Magik 3! I am one of them."

I took a bow.

No one said a word.

My dog, Cheerio, ran up to me to say hello. At least someone in the family appreciated me. I took another bow. A really deep one. A really long one.

"I'm going to my room until dinner," Emily said. "This is too strange for me."

My father was sitting in his boxers at the dining-room table, working on a crossword puzzle. He was wearing a pair of glasses on the top of his head. He does that sometimes, even though I'm pretty sure he doesn't have eyes up there. He looked at me like I was a short stranger.

"You're late," he said.

"We were with Papa Pete at McKelty's."

"You should have called."

"But I was with Papa Pete. Not some stranger," I told him.

"You have to learn to be responsible, Hank," he answered back.

Responsible? I'm a small-business owner. How much more responsible can you get? But I didn't tell my dad that.

"I'm sorry, Dad," I said. "I'll call next time."

My mother came in from the kitchen. I could tell she'd been cooking because her hair was pulled back with a hairband. Her hair is blonde and curly, and when she wears it loose, bits of the food she's cooking sometimes land in it. She's had all kinds of things in her hair – flour, chunks of chocolate-chip-cookie dough. Once, she even found a bean. The hairband is her new discovery, and it's been working really well for her.

Mum started to push my father's papers to the end of the dining-room table. We eat at one end of the table and his office is at the other. He does something with computers. I'm not sure what it is, but I know it's pretty boring.

"How was your first day, my big fourth-grader?" my mum asked, kissing me on the cheek. "Did you remember to bring home your homework sheet?"

"That would be a first," said Emily the Perfect. She came out of her bedroom carrying her iguana, Katherine, on her shoulder. Who names a lizard Katherine?

Some people say that Emily and I look alike. Even though she's fifteen months younger than me, we're almost the same size. We both have blue eyes and blond hair that goes in a lot of different directions, like my dad's. But as far as I'm concerned, that's where the similarity ends. For one thing, I don't paint each fingernail a different colour like Emily does. And for another, I don't have to use Chapstick all the time because I lick my lips too much. And most importantly, I don't walk around with an iguana on my shoulder.

My sister Emily calls herself a reptile person. I call her a *creepy* reptile person. I mean, you're trying to enjoy your dinner and all of a sudden, her iguana snaps its long tongue out and snatches a carrot off your plate. How can a guy digest? And my parents don't say anything. Not a word!

My mum went back to the kitchen and brought out some soup for dinner. It was mushroom. I could tell it was Papa Pete's recipe because it smelled great. She served everyone up a big bowl, took off her hairband and apron, and sat down at the table.

"Who wants to share their day?" Mum asked. She says this every night at dinner. The great thing is that she really wants to hear all about your day.

I let Emily start.

"Who do you think got appointed rubber monitor?" she said. "Me. And our teacher, Miss Springflower, said I have the neatest handwriting she's ever seen. And she was really impressed with my summer reading list. She said she's never met a not-even third-grader who could read a three hundred and twenty-nine page book. I think I'm her favourite, and it's only the first day."

The only thought that came to my mind was, *Could you barf?*

The iguana's elastic tongue shot out for some soup. She missed, and her tongue made the soup splash high out of the bowl, hitting my father smack in the eye.

"Emily, take that thing and put it back in your room," he said.

Finally, he was reacting in a normal way.

"This so-called thing is an iguana whose natural habitat is the Galapagos," Emily said.

"So, can we FedEx it back home?" I asked.

My father chuckled.

"Stanley," said Mum. "Katherine is a member of this family, too."

"And what am I?" said my dad. "A lowly fly on the wall?"

I love it when adults say things like that – things that sort of make sense but don't really.

"Let's not spoil a nice dinner," said my mum. She turned her attention to me. I was crumbling a cracker into my soup. I like to float the pieces, watch them get soggy and eat them just before they sink.

"Hank," said my mum. "It's your turn. Let's hear about your day."

"My teacher, Ms Adolf, is so strict," I began. "We have to write a *huge* essay about what we did in our summer holidays. Five paragraphs."

No sooner were the words out of my mouth than I knew I had made a big mistake. My father wanted to know when it was due. My mother wanted to know when I was planning to start. Knowing me, they both suggested I begin tonight.

"I want to start on it, because you know how much I believe in getting an early start on things," I said with my fingers crossed. "But tonight I have a very important meeting in the clubhouse at seven."

"Honey, you know how long it takes you to do your homework," said my mother.

"This is the first homework assignment of the year," added my father. "You have to make a good impression on your teacher."

"But my business partners are counting on me," I pleaded.

"What business partners?" my father asked, getting irritated.

"Now, Henry..." my mother said.

Uh-oh. The H-word. Whenever she calls me Henry, I know it's all over.

"We've talked about starting this school year off on the right foot. I know you want to do that, don't you?"

"But I have six whole days to write it," I said. "That's less than a paragraph a day. And this meeting could change my entire life. And yours."

"That's enough," my father said. "Right after dessert, you're going to march into your room, sit down at your desk and start writing. I want one paragraph completed tonight."

Just then, Katherine flipped out her disgusting tongue and snapped up the last piece of cracker that I'd been saving.

This night was going nowhere fast.

CHAPTER 7

I love my room and I hate my room.

My bunk bed can be turned into a fort. All I have to do is tuck the blankets under the top mattress and let them hang down to the floor. I sleep on the bottom bunk and my desk is directly opposite the window. Everything is where I want it to be. My clock radio is by my bed. My CD player is portable, so it can move to where I need it. Inside my cupboard I have a secret panel where an old cigar box holds the most important items on Earth. There's a dollar note that Mum gave me for helping to clean up our dog's poo, a red star that my first-grade teacher gave me for telling the best story, my very first Hot Wheels car – a silver Ferrari F-50 convertible that I named Shiny – a load of baseball cards that will be very valuable someday and ... that's pretty much it.

Those are the things I love about my room. What I hate about my room is that's where homework calls to me day and night like a monster. "Finish me. Finish me. Pick up your pencil."

I sat down at my desk and took out a piece of lined paper. Let's not forget that I'm allergic to lined paper. But I was determined to concentrate and get some of my essay done.

Cheerio ran into my room. He started to spin round in a circle. Now let me ask you this: how can a guy concentrate when his dog spends most of his waking hours chasing his tail? Cheerio, who is a very long dachshund, has been trying to catch his tail since he was a puppy. That's how he got his name. He's beigeish-brownish. So is a Cheerio. He looks like a circle. So does a Cheerio. Sometimes he spills his milk on himself, and then he looks like a *bowl* of Cheerios.

Watching Cheerio spin is like watching clothes twirling around in the dryer. It's boring, and you try to look away. But somehow you're just sucked in.

I was finally able to unhook my eyes from Cheerio and look at my desk. The lined paper stared up at me. My pencil was sharpened and ready. So why couldn't I just pick it up and write ... something ... anything? The piece of paper looked like it was spinning around the desktop ... like my dog. I pushed my hand straight out to stop it. My thoughts were spinning. *Niagara Falls...* I wrote that down. At last, something was coming. *My family is in raincoats and boots and rain hats. We had to rent them.* I wrote that down, too.

All of a sudden, I looked down and saw that my desk drawer was open a crack. My hand just shot down and pulled it open even further. Boy, was it a mess! How did that happen? I felt this powerful need to straighten up everything in my drawer.

My broken watch collection was all over the place. My special marbles had rolled all the way to the back. I took some Scotch tape and taped the marbles down. I was on fire! Then I noticed that the ballpoint pens had somehow got into the pencil part of the divider. I couldn't have that.

"Henry Zipzer, are you writing your essay?" my mother called from outside my door.

I slammed the drawer shut and picked up my pencil.

"You bet, Mum."

I looked down at the paper. I squinted and saw a sentence and a half – that was all I had written. I looked at my clock radio. We had a seven o'clock meeting in our clubhouse down in the basement. How was I going to make it? I'd never get out of my room. I hated my room. I hated my essay. I hated my brain. Why couldn't I think or write or spell or add or divide? Forget about multiplying.

It's not like I don't try. I do. I go over and over and over my times tables and my vocabulary lists. My sister tests me, and I know everything. But then comes the test, and I can't remember them. It's like my mind is a blackboard and the words just slide off it in the time it takes to walk from my flat to school, which is a block and a half away. It makes me so mad that sometimes I hit my head with my fist, hoping I'll start everything working again.

The piece of paper was still there in front of me. Still pretty much empty. I picked up my pencil and reread my sentence and a half. Great. I had spelled Niagara wrong. Rubbing out was a trick.

My rubber usually ripped the paper to shreds. As I moved it over the sheet of paper, a hole started to appear. Small at first, and then it grew. It finally got so big, I could see the desktop through it.

I screwed up the sheet of paper and threw it. It hit the rim of my bin. Mum and Dad gave the bin to me for my birthday last year, and they put family pictures all around the outside under plastic.

Start again, Hank, I told myself. *Think.* Niagara Falls ... or Does It? *by Hank Zipzer.*

I wondered if the title could be considered a paragraph?

Probably not.

CHAPTER 8

"**Man, are you late!**" Frankie said, a little bit angrily. "It's seven-thirty."

"We thought you weren't coming," Ashley chimed in.

"Hey, *I* didn't think I was coming," I snapped back. "Parent problems."

"I happen to know that your mum isn't even home," said Frankie. "I know that because she's upside-down in my living room."

"My dad went to yoga class tonight too," said Ashley. "He said he needed to de-stress. I'd be stressed too if I had to look at pictures of people's disgusting insides all day."

"We've got to get my dad to go to yoga," I said. "He could definitely use some de-stressing. He wouldn't let me come here tonight until I had written a paragraph of my essay."

"Did you do one?" asked Ashley.

"Yeah, I wrote a paragraph."

"Great," said Ashley, throwing an arm round me.

"Then I rubbed it out."

"Not so great." Ashley looked worried.

"I assume you didn't mention the rubbing out part to Silent Stan," said Frankie.

"He didn't ask, and I didn't tell."

I don't lie to my parents, but I have to confess, there are times when I don't tell them everything. I think you know what I mean.

I fell backwards into one of the sofas that lined the wall of our clubhouse. Cheerio, who had come with me, started to sniff the place out. He always sniffs around like he's going to find something new. He never does, but as long as he doesn't lift his leg, I figure he can do whatever he wants.

Our clubhouse is in the basement of our block of flats. When you get out of the lift, you start smelling soapsuds because the laundry room is to the right. But if you turn to the left, there are three rooms with padlocks on them filled with stuff no one in the building wants. Old chairs and sofas and bird cages, suitcases of every size, boxes of books and food magazines. A lot of parent kind of stuff.

One of the rooms doesn't have a lock so we use it for our hideout. It's a perfect meeting spot. Well, almost perfect. It would be totally perfect if Robert didn't know about it.

Ashley and Frankie had already made a list of the tricks Frankie was going to do for Papa Pete's show. It said:

1. Take nickels from nose.
2. Transform one scarf into many scarves.
3. Make thumb disappear.
4. Pull live furry thing from hat.

"Numbers one to three are no-brainers," Frankie said, "but number four isn't going to happen. We'd better face it now."

"But I promised Papa Pete," said Ashley. "I shook on it."

"Fine," said Frankie. "Then you've got to find me something live and furry."

"How about Robert?" I suggested.

"No," said Frankie. "His mother would freak out if we tried to stuff him in a hat."

Cheerio got tired of sniffing and started to chase his tail.

"Cheerio's at it again," Ashley said. "Doesn't he ever get dizzy?"

I looked at Cheerio twirling around like a top. A flash of inspiration hit me. Cheerio! He was small. He was furry. He was alive.

"Members of Magik 3," I said as I sprang off the sofa. "I have the answer. We're pulling Cheerio out of that hat."

When he heard his name, Cheerio stopped spinning for a minute and looked me right in the eye. Then he started spinning again.

Frankie put his hand to his forehead, like he had a bad headache. "He does that inside a hat and I'm telling you right now, he'll burn a hole in the fabric."

"Cheerio can be calm," I said. "He'll cooperate."

"Right, and my name is Bernice," said Frankie. "By the way, here's another question, guys. What top hat have you ever seen that this dog would fit in?"

"He's our best choice, Frankie. He's also our *only* choice," Ashley said. "So we'll just have to figure out a way." She pushed her glasses up on her nose and folded her arms in a way that meant business.

Ashley can be tough when she wants to be.

"I think we can build a hat big enough to hold Cheerio," I suggested. "There's stuff all over here that we could use."

"Yeah, like what?" Frankie asked.

I looked around. On the shelf above the door, I saw a big, round hatbox kind of thing. We pulled it down, took off the lid and put Cheerio inside. He fitted perfectly.

"Great, we'll use this," I said. "We'll cover it in black felt."

"Like we happen to have a big pile of felt lying around," Frankie said.

"I know where they sell felt." I had just seen some the week before in the ninety-nine-cent shop. It was in the school supplies section.

"It's still not going to look like a hat," said Frankie.

"Then we'll get some cardboard and make a brim," I answered.

"That sounds hard," said Ashley. "How will we get the brim to stick on?"

"Trust me," I said. "I'm a genius with super glue."

"OK, genius," said Frankie, "tell me how we're going to keep your nutcase dog inside the hat until it's time to pull him out?"

"I'll build a pocket inside and put some biscuits there to keep Cheerio calm." By now, Frankie and Ashley were pretty impressed with my ideas. I have to admit, I was too.

"We can even put the whole hat on wheels," I said. I don't know where that idea came from. It just popped into my mind. One second there was nothing in my head, and the next second there was a hat on wheels. It was amazing.

"Hank, you are covered in creativity," Ashley said.

"You're the second person today who's used that word," I said to her. "Ms Adolf told me she was looking forward to seeing me use my creativity in my essay."

Then it struck me. Creativity. It was the answer to all my problems. Creativity had solved our hat problem. And creativity was going to get me through Ms Adolf's essay. And not just get me through, either. My creativity was going to get me the best mark of my life.

Let everyone else write their stupid five paragraphs. Not me. Right then and there, I decided I was going to *build* my essay. I'd *bring* Niagara Falls into the classroom, water and all.

I could see it in my mind, just like I had seen the big hat for Cheerio. I'd build a living model of Niagara Falls, with cliffs and waterfalls and even a

boat. Everyone would know first hand what I had done in my summer holidays. Mr Love would hear about how great it was and come to our classroom just to see it. He'd call my dad and say what a great job I had done.

Papa Pete always says, "There are many roads to Rome." I used to think he was talking about the traffic in Italy. But now it made sense to me. What he meant was, if you can't get there one way, take another way. Like if you can't pull a rabbit out of a hat, pull a dachsund out. And if you can't write about Niagara Falls, *build* it.

My brain was on fire, and it felt good.

CHAPTER 9

Do you know what lucky is? Lucky is having friends who understand that building a magic hat can wait when Niagara Falls needs to be built right away. Lucky is having friends who don't make you feel stupid even though that's how you think of yourself. Lucky is having friends who don't make fun of you because some things – well, a lot of things – are hard.

I am so lucky.

As soon as I told Frankie and Ashley my idea about building Niagara Falls instead of writing the essay, they both volunteered to help.

"This is a big project," I said.

"We'd better make a list of supplies we'll need," Ashley suggested. "Frankie, you get a pencil and write the list."

"No way," he said. "I'm not a secretary. I'm a builder. A hammer-and-nails kind of guy."

"When was the last time you built anything?" Ashley asked him.

"Kindergarten," said Frankie. "Remember that awesome gingerbread house I made out of milk cartons and crackers?"

"I remember that it collapsed and then you ate it," I said.

"OK, you win. Hand me the pencil," Frankie said.

"The first thing we're going to need is water," I said. "Lots and lots of water."

"Newspaper and flour to build the cliffs," added Ashley.

"Twigs to make trees out of," I said.

"And rhinestones for the stars in the sky," said Ashley.

Frankie stopped writing.

"This isn't a T-shirt, Ashweena. Bear in mind, we are building one of the natural wonders of the world. Rhinestones have no place here."

"Then how about rocks for the cliffs," suggested Ashley.

"Rocks are good," said Frankie. He added "Rocks" to the list.

"Let's put a boat at the bottom of the falls," I said. "I must have a toy boat somewhere. And maybe I can get a spare pump from one of Emily's old fish tanks."

"What do you need a pump for?" asked Frankie.

"Something's got to push the water over the falls," I said.

"We better have a saucepan to collect the water," said Ashley. "A big saucepan."

I asked everyone to gather as much stuff as they could and meet the next night to begin building. We were all pretty excited – until we turned to leave, that is. Then we saw the worst thing you could possibly find in the doorway. Robert.

"Hi guys," he said with a grin. "Good news. My mum says I can join the meeting."

I've got to remember to tell his mother he's not invited.

"What are you guys doing?" he asked.

"Fourth-grade stuff," answered Frankie. "You wouldn't understand."

"Try me."

"We're building Niagara Falls," I said.

"More than six hundred thousand gallons of water flow over Niagara Falls every second," Robert said.

"How do you know that?" Ashley asked.

"Actually, it's all up here," Robert said, pointing to his head.

"Clear your throat, Robert," said Frankie.

Robert often gets this really annoying bubble in his throat when he talks, like he's got a little ball of spit down there. He'll just keep on talking if you don't tell him to clear that thing out.

"I bet you won't be able to create the mist," Robert went on. "Did you know that Niagara Falls produces enough mist to fill half the Grand Canyon every twenty minutes?"

Ashley thought for a minute. "As much as I hate to admit it, the mist does sound important," she whispered to me.

This gave Robert all the encouragement he

needed. "My mum has a fan she puts in the window on really hot days. We could use it to blow the water around to look like mist. I think she'd let us borrow it."

Oh great. Now it was *us*.

The next morning, I waited until Emily was in the shower and then went into her room. In her wardrobe, I found an old pump left over from when she had her Japanese fighting fish. I put the pump in a paper bag, along with a Lego boat from my toy chest. Then I went into the kitchen to find a saucepan. As I was clanking around in the cupboard, my mum came in.

"Hi honey. What are you looking for?"

"That big roasting tin you cook turkey in at Thanksgiving."

"Oh, I lent it to Mrs Fink. She was making a turkey for her son-in-law's birthday. Come to think of it, she never returned it."

"If it's OK with you, I'm going to get it back from her. I need it for a school project."

"Be sure to ask her how the turkey turned out," my mum said, as she put water on for tea. "I suggested she stuff it with wheatgrass and bean sprouts. I'm sure it was delicious."

I went next door to Flat 10B and knocked on the door. Mrs Fink answered. She isn't a small woman, and in her pink dressing gown, she looked like one of those giant pink elephants in the cartoons.

"Hankie!" she said. "Come in for a doughnut. I'll put my teeth in."

"That's OK, Mrs Fink," I said. "I have to get to school. I was just wondering if I could get our turkey tin back."

"Of course, darling," she said. She went to the kitchen and came back with the tin. As she handed it to me, Mrs Fink smiled and I thought I saw her gums. I took the tin and ran, without asking about the turkey.

After school, I took all my stuff to our clubhouse. Frankie had brought a big stack of newspapers. Ashley had a box of rocks and pebbles she had collected at Riverside Park. Even good old Robert showed up with a fan.

There's a sink in the broom cupboard down the hall, and I half filled the turkey tin with water. We let Robert do most of the newspaper shredding.

Ashley and I soaked the paper and mixed it with flour to make papier-mâché. As we built the cliffs, Ashley reminded me that we had to make a hole for the hose that was going to bring the water to the top of the falls.

The next day, we made another batch of papier-mâché and added it to the cliffs. A couple of times, the cliffs got so high that the papier-mâché slid down to the bottom. I had to prop it up while Ashley held her hair dryer up to it. Even then, it took two whole days and nights for the cliffs to dry.

Finally, the cliffs were ready for us to decorate. We put rocks and pebbles around to make them look real. Frankie had snipped some branches off the ficus tree in his living room when his mother wasn't looking. We stuck those along the top of the cliffs to look like trees.

On Saturday night, I decided it was time to add the water part. I had been collecting cardboard tubes from our flat. Three had come from rolls of paper towels and a couple of others from bathroom tissue. I love saying "bathroom tissue". It rolls off your tongue. Not like "toilet paper", which sounds too much like what it actually is.

If I do say so myself, I had come up with a great plan to get the water to the falls. I was going to connect the tubes with waterproof tape. Then I'd wrap the outside of this cardboard snake with clingfilm. We'd hook one end up to the hole we'd made in the cliffs and the other end up to the tap in the sink in our classroom. Connect the pump, turn on the water and hey presto, Niagara Falls.

"What are you doing?" asked Frankie, when he saw me wrapping the cardboard tubes in clingfilm.

I told him my brilliant plan.

"I don't know, Zip," he said, shaking his head. "Do you think that tube is going to be strong enough to hold water?

"Hey, if you can cover a bowl of watermelon with clingfilm and turn it upside down, then this will hold too," I assured him. "I tell you, water is going to sail through this baby."

On Sunday night, we had one final meeting to finish the project. I glued more trees on to the cliffs and put little Lego people into the boat. Ashley and I carefully attached the hose. We painted the cliffs brown – or, as Robert pointed out, burnt sienna. He's a real pain about vocabulary, that guy, but I have to admit, he was very helpful.

When Niagara Falls was finished, we all stood back to admire it.

"Don't move," Frankie said. "I'll be right back."

He disappeared. Two minutes later he was back, panting. He had run up six flights of stairs to his flat. When he's on a mission, Frankie never waits for the lift. He reached into his pocket and pulled out a gleaming baby-blue stone that I recognized right away. It was his best piece of turquoise from his private rock and mineral collection. Frankie put a spot of glue on it and placed the turquoise on top of the cliff.

"It's got good karma," he said.

He gave me his classic Big Dimple smile, then put out his hand. We did our secret handshake.

"You're going to knock 'em dead, Zip."

Didn't I tell you I was lucky?

CHAPTER 10

That night, it was hard to sleep because I was so excited. I couldn't wait until morning when I'd take Niagara Falls to school and show everyone my living essay.

I heard the door creak open. My mum stuck her head in.

"All set for school tomorrow?" she asked.

"Yup."

"Are you sure you've finished your essay?" she whispered.

"It couldn't be any more complete, Mum."

"Do you need me to proofread it?"

"I'm telling you, Mum, it's perfect."

"I love you," she said.

"Me too," I said.

And she closed the door.

I stared up at the ceiling. All I could think about were the incredible things that were going to happen to me after I showed Niagara Falls. I made a list in my head.

TEN INCREDIBLE THINGS THAT WILL HAPPEN AFTER EVERYONE SEES MY NIAGARA FALLS PROJECT

BY HANK ZIPZER

1. I won't get just an A on it, I'll get the highest A they've ever given in America.
2. Ms Adolf will finally smile. (I wonder if her face will crack.)
3. They'll call an assembly for everyone in the school to see my project. Newspaper reporters will come. Television stations will bring their cameras.
4. I'll interview Frankie and Ashley on television. Maybe even Robert. Hmmm ... no, not Robert.
5. The mayor of Niagara Falls will come to shake my hand.
6. Head Teacher Love will declare a school holiday in my honour.

7. I'll be called to the White House to show my project to the president.

8. The president will be so impressed, he'll pass a law that kids in the fourth grade no longer have to write essays.

9. Every fourth-grade student in the country will break their number-two pencils in half.

10. Just before they do, they will all write me letters to say thank you. I'll have to get a secretary just to answer my fanmail.

11. I will never have to clear the table again. Emily, on the other hand, will have to do it until she's fifty-six.

I fell asleep with a smile on my face.

CHAPTER 11

OK, about the list in the last chapter. You're right. There are eleven things on it and I said there were only going to be ten. Well, you shouldn't be surprised. It's me, Hank Zipzer. I'm lucky that all my fingers and toes are attached. Otherwise, I'd lose count.

When my alarm clock rang the next morning,
I didn't hear the buzzer. All I heard was, "Monday
morning, Monday morning, Monday morning."
It was going to be tricky getting Niagara Falls to
school, so we had to leave extra early. Ashley said
her mum had to be at the hospital anyway, so she
didn't mind walking us to school.

We met in the basement. Frankie and I each
picked up one end of the tin. Since it was my project,
I volunteered to be the one who walked backwards.
Ashley held the water pump, the clingfilm-wrapped
hose and a plastic bag with my costume in it.
(I haven't mentioned the costume before, because

93

I threw it in at the last minute. I thought it would add what Papa Pete calls "pizazz".)

When we got outside our building, Ashley cleared the people out of the way and kept watch for big cracks in the pavement so I wouldn't trip. First we passed Mr Kim's market. He was putting out buckets of fresh flowers for the day. When he saw Niagara Falls, he took a flower from one of the buckets and put it on the top of the cliffs.

"Flowers grow on mountain top," he said.

"Thanks, Mr Kim," I said.

We reached the corner and waited for the lights to change. When they were red, we crossed Amsterdam Avenue. A couple of taxi drivers blew their horns as we walked by, probably because they were so amazed to see Niagara Falls passing by right in front of them. I felt good because a lot of them had probably never been to Niagara Falls, and at least now they were getting a chance to see it.

"Please! Hold your honks!" I shouted, as I took a half bow. "And thank you, one and all."

Frankie started to laugh, and then I did too. Ashley knew we were heading into one of our marathon laughing fits. When we were little, she watched us get plenty of time-outs at school because of our uncontrollable laughter.

"Stop it, boys!" she said. "Concentrate. You don't want to drop it now."

"Children, don't dawdle at the junction," Ashley's mum said. She had a good point. You can't fool around at a New York junction. When the lights change, the cars go. If you're in the way, it's your problem.

Dr Wong is very nice but very quiet. Ashley says she doesn't talk much because most of the people she is around all day are asleep. She's a surgeon.

We made it to the school zebra crossing without falling, tripping or dropping the project. We only had a few more steps to go, but they were tricky ones. There are a couple of big potholes in front of our school. They're always fixing them, but then other ones pop up. I heard once that potholes happen in the winter when there is ice and snow. Or maybe it's the traffic. No, I think it's the weather. When Emily was in kindergarten, I told her they were dragon footprints. Of course, it didn't scare her because, as we all know, she likes reptiles.

Our school is three storeys high. On the street side of the building, the bricks are covered with a big mural that was painted by some local New York artists. It shows a lot of kids with books open, sitting and reading happily under a rainbow. They sure didn't use me as a model.

When the road was clear, Mr Baker, the lollipop man, took us across.

"That's a mighty fine looking mountain you got there," he said to us.

"It's Niagara Falls, sir," I said.

"Well, it's a mighty fine looking Niagara Falls."

That made me feel good. Even though Mr Baker says nice things to all the kids, I like to think he really did like our project.

Finally, we reached the main door of PS 87. There were kids swarming all around the school, and we had to be careful not to get crunched. We were attracting a lot of attention.

"Keep your distance," I said to a bunch of first-graders who were hovering around us. "Important fourth-grade business coming through."

Ashley held the door open for us and we backed

into the corridor. We started the long climb to the second floor and our classroom. As luck would have it, the first person we saw when we got to the top was Nick McKelty.

"What is *that* supposed to be?" he asked in his usual creepoid manner.

I wasn't going to let this guy get to me.

"You just might be the only person in New York not to get it," I said. "We totally stopped traffic on Amsterdam Avenue. The taxis honked like we were a float in the Thanksgiving Day parade."

"Oh yeah?" McKelty said. "I was asked to ride on a float this year."

"Right, and my name is Bernice," Frankie said.

"In fact," McKelty went on, "they wanted me to be Santa Claus in the parade, but I said, 'Sorry, I'm already booked. Maybe next year.'"

"Breathe," Frankie said to himself. Then he turned to McKelty. "That's good," he said, "because your face would've scared all those little kids. It's such a drag seeing kids cry at a parade."

"Oh yeah?" McKelty answered.

"What a comeback," said Ashley. "You're quick, McKelty."

From around the corner, we heard the *squeak, squeak, squeak* of rubber on lino. That could only be Head Teacher Love. He always wears these black rubber-soled shoes that do up with two Velcro straps. I guess he has never learned to tie his laces.

"What have we here?" he boomed in his tall-man-bushy-hair voice.

We put Niagara Falls down on the floor.

"My summer holiday," I answered.

Nick stepped right in front of me.

"Our assignment is to do a five-paragraph essay on what we did this summer," said Nick. He gave Mr Love a smile that any sane person would describe as very, very icky. "*My* adventure was so exciting that *my* essay turned out to be *eight* paragraphs. And that's cutting it down from ten."

"Mr McKelty, you've got a future." Mr Love grinned. Then he turned to me. "And as for you, Mr Zipzer, don't be late for class."

He squeaked off down the hall. McKelty ran after him, continuing to blab in his ear – probably telling him how much he happens to love Velcro straps on shoes.

"Don't be late," I muttered under my breath. "Where does he think I'm going? To the dining room for a big breakfast?"

"Forget him," said Ashley. "You've got to keep your mind on what you're doing here."

I could still see McKelty walking down the hallway, talking to Mr Love like he was his best friend. Then I saw something truly disgusting.

"I don't believe it," I said. "McKelty's putting his arm round him!"

The McKelty Factor strikes again.

The bell rang and Nick came lumbering down the corridor towards us. Just before he turned into the classroom, he stopped and looked at me.

"I have a wonderful surprise in store for you, Zippity Zipzer," he said.

He gave me an annoying flick under the chin and slithered into class like the slimy snake he is.

CHAPTER 13

Ms Adolf was on the prowl. She was hungry for paper. "Please take your essays out, class," she said. "I hope you remembered to staple them in the upper-left-hand corner."

She walked up and down the aisles, clutching her register close to her chest. When she stopped at my desk, I could feel her hot breath on my head.

"Your desk appears to be empty, Mr Zipzer," she said.

My heart was pounding. This was the moment.

"I thought we agreed you were to read your essay first," she snapped.

"And I am completely, totally prepared, Ms Adolf," I said.

I looked at Frankie. I gave him a nod. He gave Ashley a nod. The three of us stood and went to our planned positions.

Ashley took the clingfilm-wrapped tube and attached it with tape to the tap at the sink. Frankie and I disappeared into the corridor.

"Excuse me!" Ms Adolf shouted. I think she was starting to get angry.

I stuck my head back into the classroom and said, "Get ready for creativity like you've never seen before."

Out in the corridor, we got my costume out of the plastic bag. Frankie held the yellow raincoat for me to slip into and I pulled on the boots and the fisherman's hat. Then we picked up the project and walked it into the classroom, where we placed it by the sink.

"Exactly what do you think you're doing?" Ms Adolf demanded to know.

"What you're about to see, Ms Adolf, is what I did in my summer holidays. My living essay."

The kids moved closer so they could see. Ryan Shimozato even stood up on his chair. Katie Sperling and Kim Paulson were whispering to each other and giggling. I noticed that Nick McKelty kept looking at the door to the classroom, like he was expecting someone.

Before Ms Adolf could object again, I began.

"Niagara Falls was formed twelve thousand years ago, but when I visited this summer, it didn't look a day over eleven thousand. It did, however, look wet – really wet."

That was Ashley's cue. She turned on the tap at the sink. With a quick twist of the nozzle, the water started to run through our hose and into the hole at the top of the papier-mâché cliff. I was so excited I couldn't continue. The falls were actually doing what they were supposed to do ... falling! The water hitting the bottom of the turkey tin sounded like rain.

Ashley turned on the fish tank pump and it started to bubble, moving the water from the bottom of the turkey tin back up to the top of the falls. The boat at the bottom of the tin rose in the water. It was floating! Everything was working!

"Seven hundred and fifty thousand gallons of water flow over these falls every second," I said. Old Robert had finally come in handy.

"Do you see that boat?" I asked, pointing to the Lego people in it. "Picture my mother, my father, my sister and me – dressed as I am now, covered with mist."

At that moment, Frankie turned on the fan, and a little of the water started to blow towards my raincoat. The kids gasped.

"Awesome," said Ryan Shimozato.

"Truly awesome," said Justin, Ricky and Gerald. They're Ryan's crew and they like whatever he likes.

"Half the falls are in Canada, and the other half are in the United States, making Niagara Falls a link between our two countries," I went on. I remembered the tour guide had said that while we were waiting in line to get on the boat. I was on a roll. I knew so many facts about Niagara Falls, I could've gone on until lunch or longer.

Out of the corner of my eye, I saw that Frankie was trying to get my attention. I glanced over at him. He whispered something, but I couldn't quite understand him. It sounded like "no peeking". I didn't know what he was talking about. I shrugged and went on.

"We left New York City on a muggy August morning," I said, pretending to be driving in a car. "My mother said it was so hot you could fry eggs on her knees."

The kids laughed. They were loving this. I really felt wonderful and successful. *Maybe I'll be a stand-up comedian when I grow up,*

I thought. *Take this show on the road.* I looked at Frankie. He wasn't laughing. Why not?

Whatever he had been trying to say to me, he said again. "No peeking"? Was that it? I still couldn't understand him. He sure was flapping his arms around a lot.

Just then, the door swung open. In walked Leland Love. Wow, this was great. The head teacher *was* coming to see my project, just like I had hoped.

"Tourists from all over the world come to see Niagara Falls," I said. I was getting more and more confident by the minute. "A couple from Italy asked me to take their picture with the falls in the background," I added. I hadn't even planned to tell that part of the story. It just came out.

Suddenly, Frankie walked in front of me and with an Italian accent said, "I thinka thesa falls are betta than SpaghettiOs."

The class howled.

"SpaghettiOs rule!" Luke Whitman laughed. "SpaghettiOs forget-ios!" It doesn't take much for Luke to go out of control.

"What are you doing?" I whispered to Frankie. "You weren't supposed to talk."

"I've been trying to tell you," Frankie whispered. "We're leaking! Look!"

I looked over at the hose. Oh no, this wasn't happening. The cardboard was soaking wet. The tube was turning to mush and the last piece of tape holding the hose to the cliffs was coming loose. I yelled for Ashley to turn off the water. She ran to the sink, but she was so nervous, she turned the water on full force instead, which totally blew the hose off the project. Water sprayed everywhere, but mostly on Ms Adolf. She opened her mouth to speak and got a mouthful of falls.

The hose started to spin around, and the kids all ran for cover, laughing and shouting. Ms Adolf was so stunned, she just stood there. *Bam!* She got pelted again with a blast of water. When she put her hands up to her face to block the water, her register fell to the floor. It landed in a puddle of water. She gasped and tried to reach for it, but Luke Whitman was running wild and stamped on it, pushing it completely underwater.

Ms Adolf stared at her register. The paper was absorbing water fast and turning into a soggy mess.

She opened her mouth wide, like she was going to scream really loudly, but all that came out was a mouse-like "eeeeekkk".

Bam! The hose came around again and hit her with another shot of water. She was really

wet now. It looked like she had just stepped out of the shower with her clothes on. The pile of grey hair that was always neatly pinned on top of her head fell down and looked like a horse's tail.

"The water!" Mr Love yelled. "Someone turn

off the water!" The kids were all laughing pretty hard, so no one moved towards the sink. Mr Love bolted across the room. He had to push past Luke Whitman, who was leading a bunch of kids in a rain dance. There was so much water on the floor, the classroom looked like a pond. Pencils, crayons, Ms Adolf's register and even a tuna fish sandwich in a bag floated by.

Mr Love sloshed over to the sink. As he reached the counter, he stepped on the bag. It exploded and the tuna sandwich squished out from under his shoe. It was a slippery mess. Mr Love went sliding on the sandwich like he was on water skis. The last thing I saw before he went swimming was his hand reaching for the counter with the turkey tin on it. As the tin tipped, the papier-mâché flew and the muddy, mushy Niagara Falls landed with a splat all over Mr Love's face.

I didn't mean to laugh, but I couldn't stop. In fact, I was laughing so hard that I fell bum-first into the water. Then what do I see but Nick McKelty's hand reaching out to Mr Love.

"Don't worry, sir," he said. "I'll save you."

Sometimes I think things happen the way they're

supposed to, because Nick McKelty, suck-up of the century, slipped too and went flying headfirst into the muck. When he came up for air, he looked like he had a papier-mâché chicken sitting on his head. He wiped his face and leaned over to Head Teacher Love.

"Didn't I tell you Zipzer was about to launch a disaster?" he said.

Oh, so *that's* why Head Teacher Love had come to class. McKelty, that rat, had told him to come and see me make a fool of myself. And stupid me thought it was because he had heard I had a great project.

Head Teacher Love didn't say a word. All he did was wag a finger at me. I knew what that meant.

"I'll see you in my office … now!"

CHAPTER 14

The corridor is a lonely place when you're sitting on the bench outside the head teacher's office. Kids you know walk by on the way to the toilets or the water fountain, but no one says hello to you. No one even looks at you. It's like you're wearing a sign round your neck that says TROUBLE – KEEP AWAY.

I had been waiting in the corridor for more than an hour. They were inside – the three of them, Mr Love and the Zipzers. That would be Stan and Randi. Also known as Mum and Dad.

It was hard to sit still. I got up and asked Mrs Crock in the attendance office if I could have a pencil and paper, just to doodle or something.

"You're supposed to be using this time to think about what you've done," she said.

"I think better when I doodle," I told her.

"So do I," she said. She gave me a piece of paper and her pencil. That was nice of her.

When I went back into the corridor, Mr Love was standing outside his office. He didn't speak – he just wagged his finger, inviting me in. It's the kind of invitation you don't say no to.

As I entered the office, I could tell my father was really angry. I knew that because his bum was hovering above the chair cushion, not quite touching it.

"Can I say something?" I said.

"Absolutely not," answered Mr Love. "I think your actions have spoken loudly enough."

I noticed that Mr Love's office smelled a little like tuna. *It must be from his shoes,* I thought. He had changed his shirt, but he still had some papier-mâché stuck to his cheek. It was right above his Statue of Liberty mole. I couldn't help thinking that the Statue of Liberty finally had a torch.

"What you did today in class was completely irresponsible," Mr Love said.

I turned to my father. He would understand. "But, Dad, what I was trying to do—"

My father stood up. "Are you aware of the chaos you have created, Hank? First of all, you didn't follow the rules. You can't just make up your own assignment."

"Yes, but I wanted to—"

"Don't interrupt your father," my mother said. I couldn't believe it. Even Mum was on their side. I thought maybe it was the shoes. She usually wears sandals, but she had put on her black leather loafers, the ones that look like Ms Adolf's shoes. She's not as much fun when she wears those shoes.

"You were supposed to write an essay. Five paragraphs. That's with a pencil, Hank. Not papier-mâché." My father was seriously mad.

"But, Dad, I remembered every fact I learned on our trip. I was writing it with my mouth. Like, did you know that Niagara Falls is two thousand two hundred and twenty feet wide, and it's one hundred and seventy-three feet high, and—"

"Enough of this," interrupted Mr Love. "We are here to decide on an appropriate punishment for what you've done."

At this moment I realized that the president of the United States was not going to be inviting me to the White House.

"Detention for two weeks," Head Teacher Love said.

"Grounded at home," my father added. "Same length of time."

My brain froze. Two weeks! The magic show – oh no! The magic show was right in the middle of my punishment.

I'm dead. I'm doomed. I'm out of the Magik 3.

CHAPTER 15

I left Head Teacher Love's office and headed downstairs to the dining room. A couple of first-graders passed me on their way to the library.

"I think that's the boy who got into trouble," one of them whispered loudly. They stared at me like I had just robbed a bank or something. I spilled a little water on the floor. Big deal. OK, a lot of water. OK, a *whole* lot of water.

What does a guy do in this situation? I figured the only thing to do was wave. I went into my best Hank Zipzer strut.

"Good to see you," I said, grinning at them. "What's up in show-and-tell today?"

I think I scared them because they ran away. I continued downstairs. Some kids were already leaving the dining room and heading out to the playground. I passed Ryan and Gerald. Ryan held up his hand for a high five.

"You're a riot, man," he said.

"Truly," said Justin and Ricky, who were following behind.

"Your buddies are still eating lunch at your usual spot," Ryan said, pointing in the general direction of our table.

I went over to the table and slid in next to Ashley. She was in the middle of telling Frankie and Robert how she was going to spend her money from the magic show.

"I already have nine dollars saved," she was saying. "With the ten dollars we'll each earn, I'll have enough to get the dolphin which will complete my crystal sea family."

"I'd hold off on that dolphin," I said.

"How bad was Mr Love?" Frankie asked. "Paint the picture, Zip."

"It was ugly," I answered. "I didn't get one word in. What I did get was two weeks of detention at school and two weeks of being grounded at home."

"With or without TV?" asked Frankie.

"That is without any electronic device known to mankind," I said.

Frankie grabbed his heart and fell to the ground. "Just the thought of it makes me stop breathing."

"Of course they're going to let you out for the magic show," Ashley said. She was twirling her ponytail in her fingers, which she does when she's worried.

"No," I answered. I didn't have the courage to look at her. "They said no exceptions."

"I can take his place," Robert chimed in.

"No, you can't," we answered together.

As if what was happening wasn't bad enough, suddenly a dark cloud appeared. Its name was Nick McKelty.

"Oh, poor thing, did Head Teacher Love bust you hard?" the big creep said in this stupid baby voice. His teeth were looking especially wonky.

"Hank got two weeks' detention," Robert volunteered. As you've probably already noticed, Robert doesn't know when to keep his mouth shut.

"What are you going to do about your grandpa's magic show at my dad's bowling alley?" Nick said. "Sounds like it's not happening." He was really enjoying this.

Before I had a chance to answer, he threw his big, slimy arm round me. He put his face up to mine, and there it was – the bad breath again. I didn't breathe.

"Hey, don't worry about it, Zipper man," he said. "I got you covered."

"*You*?" I said, taking a breath and removing his arm from my shoulder. "What can *you* do, McKelty?"

"I'll put on a bowling show. I'll knock down more pins than ... than ... than..." I could see him searching for something clever to say, but as usual, he came up empty.

"I'll knock down a whole lot of pins," he finally spat out. "I just have to decide if I should use my left hand or my right hand."

"For your information," said Ashley, "the bowling league doesn't want to see *bowling*. They know how to do that. They want to see *magic*. That's why they hired us."

"My ball handling *is* magical," McKelty said. He was really happy with that comeback. He reached over and in one swipe his apelike hand nabbed Robert's Jelly swirl and Ashley's Nestlé Crunch right off the table.

"Don't feel bad," he said as he walked away. "There's always next year."

We were silent. We didn't feel bad. We felt horrible.

"Hey, come on, guys," I said with fake cheerfulness. "You can do the show without me!"

"We can't build the hat without you," said Ashley. "You're the one who knows how to do everything."

"Besides, who do you think is going to get Cheerio inside the hat?" asked Frankie. "Do you think that dog is going to listen to me? Not in this century."

I knew they were right. I had ruined everything for them.

I told them I was sorry.

But I don't think it helped.

CHAPTER 16

The bell rang at three o'clock. Everyone grabbed their rucksacks and headed for the door. They were on their way to football practice or sax lessons or other fun after-school activities. But not me. Nope. I was about to start my first day of detention. It was going to be me in a chair and Ms Adolf at her desk for the next fun-filled hour.

I must have really sighed loudly.

"Do you have something to say?" Ms Adolf asked.

I didn't say a word. I made a sound. The human body does that sometimes.

"Henry," Ms Adolf said, "I assume you want to use this time wisely."

"Yes, Ms Adolf," I answered. I couldn't imagine Ms Adolf having a first name. Maybe her friends just call her Ms Adolf.

"I've decided to have you write your essay under my supervision," she said. "Using paper and pencil, Henry. No monkey business this time."

I don't know why people always think monkey business is a bad thing. I love monkeys. They always seem to have such a good time, picking bugs off one another and eating them.

I took out a piece of paper and stared at it. It was blank. *So* blank. Ms Adolf sat down at her desk and began to write in her brand-new register. Neither one of us made a sound. It was so quiet, I could hear her breathing.

The clock on the wall clicked and the big hand jerked forward. One minute down, fifty-nine to go. Suddenly, the classroom door flew open and a messenger from the office came in. She handed Ms Adolf a note and disappeared just as quickly. After Ms Adolf had read the note, she got her handbag out of the bottom drawer.

"I have an emergency that I have to deal with," she said. Her pet fire-breathing dragon must be sick.

"My husband's car won't start and I have to pick him up from work."

Husband? Someone married her? No way. Do you think he kisses her goodnight?

I must have wrinkled up my face, because Ms Adolf said, "What's the face for, Henry?"

"Umm … I was just thinking about … umm … how it would feel for a raisin to try to lift up an elephant," I said.

"You would do better to keep your mind on your work, Henry, and not fill your head with silly thoughts." Ms Adolf put the register in the top drawer and locked it with her shiny key. She scribbled a note on a Post-it and gave it to me.

"The office has arranged for you to spend the rest of the hour in the music room with Mr Rock, the music teacher. He's on his way. Go there and give him this note. Sit quietly until he arrives."

The music room is in the basement. Even though it's right next to the dining room, I don't go there unless I have to. Being there makes me remember my second-grade choir audition, which I've been trying to forget ever since it happened. That was when Mrs Peacock, the music teacher, told me that if I wanted to be in the choir, I couldn't sing out loud. I was only allowed to mouth the words so I wouldn't throw everyone else off key. Mrs Peacock left last year to have a baby. I had never met Mr Rock. He was new.

The first things I noticed when I went into the music room were the posters all around the walls. Most of them were of composers – Beethoven and Mozart and all those old guys. But there were other posters too – cool ones. Pink Floyd. A super-sized photo of Manhattan from the air. An action shot of Michael Jordan going up for a tomahawk dunk. And my favourite, a picture of the coolest 1959 red-and-white Corvette you've ever seen.

A whole bunch of instruments were spread out in the room. There were triangles and xylophones and a piano. I sat down in a chair facing a set of silver-and-burgundy drums. I realized that my leg was bouncing up and down, about a mile a minute. It does that sometimes when I'm supposed to be sitting still.

As I sat there, it hit me that I had two whole weeks of misery in front of me. It didn't seem fair.

I was being punished for trying to do my best.

Thoughts started coming from every corner of my brain. I wished Mr Love had let me finish just one sentence. I wished my parents had given me a chance to tell them how much I know about Niagara Falls. I wished I was as smart as my sister. She could do anything. She has just toilet-trained her parakeet. My parents are always so proud of her.

I picked up one of the drumsticks and tapped the big drum. It felt good. I liked the sound. I hit it again, a little louder. Then I picked up the other stick and looked around to make sure I was still alone. *Bam!* I hit the drum, first with one stick, then the other. *Bam, bam, bam.* The drums were starting to sound like I felt.

Bam. I wish I didn't always forget my rucksack.

Bam. I wish I could do long division.

Bam. I wish I didn't feel so stupid all the time.

Before I knew it, I was hitting the drums so fast I could hardly see my hands. The cymbal was right in front of me. Why not? I hit it. *Clash.* The sound vibrated all around the room. I smacked it again. Now back to the drums. *Bam, clash, boom!*

"That's for detention!" I shouted.

Clash, boom, bam!

"That's for always getting into trouble!" My voice rang out.

Bam, bam, bammitty bam!

"That's five, one for each paragraph I can't write!"

Bam, boom, bam, boom, bam, boom, boom!

"And that's for my stupid brain!" I yelled.

From behind me, I heard a man's voice say, "I bet your brain isn't stupid."

I froze, then slowly turned round. The man in the doorway had a young face but a head full of curly, silver hair. He was wearing a blue denim shirt and a tie with musical notes on it.

"Mr Rock?" I asked.

"That's me," he answered. "Does your band have a CD out yet?"

"I'm really sorry," I said. "I know I wasn't supposed to touch these, but—"

"They're instruments," Mr Rock said. "They're here to play. Sounds like they helped you express yourself."

"I've had a bad day," I said.

"Because of your stupid brain?" he asked.

"Yeah. How did you know?"

"Because you just said it," he said with a smile. "It was hard to miss."

I handed Mr Rock the note from Ms Adolf.

He read it, then pulled up a chair and sat down backwards on it. I assumed he was going to ask me why I was in detention, but he didn't.

"So your name is Henry Zipzer?" he said.

"My friends call me Hank."

"Hank, that's a good name," he said. "Ever heard of Hank Aaron?"

"April the eighth, 1974," I answered. "The day Hammerin' Hank beat Babe Ruth's home-run record."

"I'm a baseball fan, too," he said. "I don't suppose you know what number home run Hank Aaron hit on that day."

"Seven hundred and fifteen. Do you want to know a weird Hank Aaron fact?"

"Sure," said Mr Rock.

"In four of his twenty-three seasons in baseball, Hank Aaron hit exactly forty-four home runs, which was his uniform number. Pretty amazing, huh?"

"Seems to me," said Mr Rock, "that your brain isn't as stupid as you think. It's got plenty of good information tucked inside it."

"I don't have a problem remembering interesting

facts," I explained. "I just can't do a lot with them. Like writing essays and spelling are tough – stuff that's easy for everyone else."

"Everybody learns differently," he said. "*Your* brain is *your* brain. You just have to figure out the right way to feed it."

"I gave it a lot of Cocoa Pops this morning," I said.

"How about music?" He laughed. "Do you ever feed it music?"

He actually waited for an answer.

"No," I said.

Mr Rock rubbed his hands together as though he was about to eat something delicious.

"I'll make a deal with you," he said. "Ms Adolf's note says you're supposed to work on your essay. We've got forty-five minutes of detention left. Let's take a few minutes to listen to some music. It might put you in the writing mood. What do you like?"

"Well, my essay is supposed to be about Niagara Falls."

"Let me see if I can find some water music," he said. "What does Niagara Falls sound like?"

"It sounded like thunder when I was there."

He shuffled through some CDs and picked one out.

"This is part of the Grand Canyon Suite," he said. "It's called *Cloud Burst*." He put it on, then turned it up loud. It really felt as though it was raining right there in the basement of PS 87. I'm not kidding.

Papa Pete says that you never know where good luck is going to come from. In my case, it came from Big Harry's Auto and Body Shop, which took the entire week to fix Mr Adolf's car. Ms Adolf had to leave early every day to pick up her husband, so I got to spend one whole week of detention with Mr Rock.

He taught me how to play "Hey Jude" on the xylophone. We looked at magazine pictures of our favourite cars. I picked the Ferrari F-50 convertible and he picked a 1947 Ford Woody with a surfboard on top. He put me in complete charge of trimming the dead leaves off his indoor plants. I liked that job.

We worked on my essay too. When I got stuck, which was every other second of every other minute, he'd ask me questions like "How did the falls make you feel?" or "What did you like best about the trip?" That really helped me focus.

The best part was listening to music. He'd put on a CD and then we'd just sit back and let music fill the room.

It felt so good, I couldn't believe I was at school.

CHAPTER 17

"**What's a nine-letter French word** for eggplant?" my father shouted to no one in particular.

I was sitting at the other end of the dining-room table, doodling in my maths workbook. As part of my punishment, my parents had taken away my privacy privileges. I wasn't allowed to do my homework in my bedroom. The worst part was having to listen to my father's crossword puzzle questions. I don't get it. What's the point of doing crossword puzzles if you have to ask everyone else for the answers?

Emily walked out of her bedroom with Katherine on her shoulder. Her long tongue was darting in and out of her mouth – Katherine's tongue, that is, not Emily's.

"Has anyone seen Katherine's bag of dinner pellets?" Emily asked.

"I put them in the cookie jar, honey," Mum called from the kitchen.

"Mum!" I yelled. "I ate those for my snack this afternoon. I thought they were one of your new healthy treats."

Emily laughed. Katherine jiggled up and down on her shoulder.

"It's not funny," I said. "Now I'll probably grow a long, disgusting iguana tongue."

As I was rinsing my mouth out at the kitchen sink, the doorbell rang.

"I'll get it!" I yelled.

"Remember to look through the spyhole first," Mum reminded me.

If I stand on my toes, I can just about get my eye up to the spyhole. I looked out but didn't see anyone.

"Who is it?" I shouted through the door.

"It's us," Frankie whispered. "Open up, Zip."

I pressed my face up against the crack in the door. "I'm grounded," I whispered back. "You know I can't play."

"We're not here to see you," Frankie said. "We're here to talk to your dad."

I opened the door. Frankie and Ashley marched right past me, with Robert bringing up the rear.

"Good evening, Mr Z.," Frankie said, going right up to my father.

"We've come to discuss a very important business matter," added Ashley.

My father looked up from his crossword puzzle.

"You kids aren't supposed to be here," he said.

"Hank is still grounded for another week."

"This matter can't wait," said Ashley.

"Aubergine," said Robert, looking at the newspaper in my father's hand.

"What's that supposed to mean?" snapped Frankie.

"It means eggplant in French," said Robert, pointing at the blank spaces on my father's crossword puzzle. "Thirteen across is *aubergine*."

"Sometimes you scare me," Frankie said to Robert.

"Come on, boys, let's not forget why we're here," Ashley said. She turned to my father, with her no-nonsense face on. "Mr Zipzer, as you know, Magik 3 has a contract with Papa Pete to put on a fantastic magic show this weekend at McKelty's Roll 'N Bowl. We've tried all week to build the special hat we need for the grand finale. But our hat looks like a sofa."

"We're begging you, Mr Z.," said Frankie. "We're *pleading* with you. Free Hank. We can't make the hat without him."

My father shook his head no.

"I'll help you with forty-three down," Robert offered. "Oh, I also happen to know three across."

"I'm afraid Hank has to learn his lesson," my father interrupted. "There'll be other magic shows."

He stood up, went to the front door and held it open. You couldn't get a much more final "no" than that. Frankie, Ashley and Robert left. My father closed the door and started back to his chair. The doorbell rang again. My father span round and yanked the door open.

"Now listen, kids," he began. Then he stopped suddenly. The next thing I heard was him saying, "I'm sorry, can I help you?"

I got up to see who was at the front door.

What is Mr Rock doing here? Oh no. I bet I broke the drum and he's here to tell my parents. I hit myself on the forehead with my fist. Not hard, but like I do sometimes when I'm frustrated with myself. How could I have been so stupid?

"I hope I'm not interrupting your dinner," Mr Rock said. "I'm Donald Rock, the music teacher from PS 87. I was wondering if I could talk to you for a moment?"

My father opened the door wider and led Mr Rock into the living room.

I was surprised to see him. I had never had a teacher pop by before. But then again, Mr Rock wasn't like other teachers.

"What's he doing here?" Emily whispered to me. "You must have messed up big-time."

My mother came out of the kitchen, drying her hands on a green checked tea towel. She picked up a plate from the dining-room table and offered Mr Rock a cracker with some of her new soy cheddar cheese spread. He popped it into his mouth before I had a chance to warn him. His lips stuck together when he tried to talk.

"I had the pleasure of spending last week with your son during his detention," Mr Rock began. He scraped some of the soy cheese off the roof of his mouth, trying to smile at the same time. My mother offered him another cracker but, smart guy that he is, Mr Rock said no thanks.

"I've had a lot of time to talk to Hank and to observe him. I've noticed that he is somewhat frustrated about his schoolwork," he said.

"Very frustrated," my mother added.

"Mr and Mrs Zipzer, I believe Hank might benefit from being tested – to see if he has any learning difficulties." Mr Rock waited for their answer.

"There's nothing wrong with Hank," my father said. "If he spent as much time doing his schoolwork as he does daydreaming and mooching around his room and building things, he'd be an *A* student. Hank is just lazy."

"Maybe that's not the case," Mr Rock said.

"You know, many children have learning difficulties. Every child's brain is wired differently."

Every brain is wired differently? What was he saying? That my brain is messed up? Oh that's great. Now everyone really will think I'm stupid!

"What does that mean, 'wired differently'?" my mum asked.

"Different kids learn in different ways," Mr Rock said. "I know that because I myself had difficulty at school."

"Hank's sister, Emily, is an excellent student," my father said. "She doesn't seem to have any problems at school."

Emily held an iguana pellet in the palm of her hand. Katherine whipped out her long tongue and snapped it up. I'll tell you one thing – Emily may not have school problems, but she has weird taste in pets.

"I'm sure you're very proud of Emily," Mr Rock continued, "but having a sister who excels adds to the pressure on Hank."

"What pressure?" said my father. "Hank doesn't worry about anything. *That's* his problem."

My mother was studying me very carefully.

My leg was bouncing up and down again. She was watching it.

"Stan, can we at least talk about this?" she asked.

"I think that's a good idea," Mr Rock said. "You have a lot to think about. I just thought it was better to have this conversation in person rather than on the phone. Give me a call if you want to talk further."

Mr Rock turned to me. "Hank, we've been talking *about* you but not *to* you. Do you have any questions?"

"Just one," I said. "Let's say a person in the fourth grade might have learning difficulties. And that person wanted to do something that was very creative, like for example a magic show, which included earning, let's say, a ten-dollar bill. Don't you think that person should be allowed to do it because he tries so hard at everything?"

"I think creativity should always be encouraged." Mr Rock smiled.

He stood up to go. He shook hands with everybody, including Katherine. She must have liked him too, because her tongue shot out and gave his hand a sticky lick.

As soon as Mr Rock had gone, I turned to my parents.

"You wouldn't go against the advice of a teacher, would you?" I asked. I had great hope in my heart. "Please … can I just do the magic show?"

My mother and father looked at each other for what seemed like a year and a half.

"We'll get back to you on this," my father finally answered.

CHAPTER 18

They got back to me the next morning.

They said yes.

The show was on!

Magik 3 was back in business. I was so excited that if you hold this book to your ear, you can hear me jumping up and down.

CHAPTER 19

At exactly seven o'clock on Saturday night, we pushed the giant hat through the swing doors of McKelty's Roll 'N Bowl. If I do say so myself, the hat was awesome. It was big and black and it had wheels. We had even built the secret pocket inside where Cheerio could hide until it was time to pull him out. To keep him happy, we put doggie treats inside the pocket with him.

McKelty's was jammed with people. It was opening night for the bowling league season. There were twelve teams. Each had their own lane and their own T-shirts. Papa Pete and The Chopped Livers were on lane five warming up. In the middle of the bowling alley, where they usually serve pizza at birthday parties, my mum had put out sandwiches. Papa Pete had warned her that anything with soy was out of the question. It had to be the real thing. I could smell the hot pastrami on fresh rye bread. My mouth started to water, but I knew we had more important things to do before we ate.

"Attention, bowlers," came a voice from the loudspeaker. I knew that voice.

"Magik 3 couldn't be with us tonight because one of its members was grounded for being too stupid to write his essay," the voice said.

The McKelty Factor strikes again.

"Instead we have something much better – a thrilling, unbelievable, death-defying bowling exhibition that stars me."

Trust Nick McKelty to put together a show starring only himself.

"That slimy toad thinks he's taking our spot," Ashley said.

"Yeah, well, I hope that slimy toad can swim because I'm going to flush him down the toilet," Frankie growled.

The loudspeaker crackled again. "For my first

feat, I'm going to bowl a strike with my left hand. Blindfolded."

Before we knew it, Nick appeared on lane ten. The jerk was actually wearing a blindfold. Everyone watched as he brought the ball up to his chest. On his bowling ball was a big picture of his slimy face. Unbelievable!

He took one, two, three steps towards the line and let the ball fly off his fingers. It landed on the lane with a *thud* and rolled smack into the gutter. The crowd groaned. I knew this was our opportunity.

I jumped up on to one of the benches and said, "Ladies and gentlemen, how about that Nick McKelty, the bowling whizz – doesn't he look great in a blindfold? Let's give it up for him."

Everyone laughed. I motioned for Frankie and Robert to wheel out the hat.

Nick looked stunned. He tried to take off his blindfold, but he had tied the knot too tightly.

"While we're setting up for the real entertainment, take a moment to enjoy the mouth acrobatics of Miss Ashley Wong, as she tries to tie not one but *two* cherry stems into a knot, never once using her hands," I said with pride.

I handed Ashley two cherries from the bar. She popped them into her mouth, scrunching up her face and moving her tongue a mile a minute. As she worked, she strolled around the audience, showing off her T-shirt with the red rhinestone cherries. By the time she got back to where she had begun, she had produced two knotted cherry stems, connected at the top. They looked like a small Christmas tree. Papa Pete led the applause.

Frankie gave me the nod. He was ready to go.

"Now, ladies and gentlemen, for the main event, I'm happy to present the freestyling magic of Frankie Townsend and Magik 3," I announced.

"Hey, what about my bowling tricks?" Nick McKelty shouted. He had finally managed to untie his blindfold. His eyes looked blazing mad. "I'm not finished yet."

"Yes, you are!" the crowd yelled back.

Nick ran into his father's office to sulk.

Frankie started right away on his act. He pulled scarves from his sleeve, cut a rope into three pieces and put it back together and pushed a pencil through the centre of a quarter that he borrowed from Papa Pete. That truly is one of my favourite tricks. And Frankie, that rat, won't tell me how he does it.

Ashley and Robert wheeled out the hat while I kept watch on Cheerio, trying to keep him calm. He was getting that look in his eye, his pre-spinning look.

"Not now, Cheerio," I whispered to him, reaching into the hat to scratch him between the ears. He loves that. "Don't go crazy on me, boy."

"And now, for my grand finale," announced Frankie. "At the special request of Papa Pete, I will pull a small live furry thing from this magical top hat!"

"It's probably a stuffed teddy bear," McKelty shouted from the office doorway. "I'm sure everyone would rather see me throw a strike backwards, between my legs, again using my left hand. Wouldn't you?"

It was his father who gave him the answer everyone else was thinking.

"Be quiet, Nick," he said, "and enjoy the show."

"Here we have a hat," Frankie began, pointing to our giant top hat. "My assistants will show you the inside of the hat." Ashley and I tipped the hat forward so everyone could see inside. Cheerio was tucked in his secret pocket so you couldn't see him. I thought I heard a tiny yip as he slid against the side.

"Notice that it's actually empty," Robert said with this kind of goofy smile. We had decided to give him a line.

"I will now take my cape and cover the hat," Frankie said. He showed the audience both sides of the cape and laid it over the hat like a tablecloth. The place was silent, except if you stood close enough to the hat, you could hear the *crunch, crunch, crunch* of doggie treats inside Cheerio's mouth.

"Hank, the magic words, if you please," Frankie said.

I stepped forward, closed my eyes and waved my hands over the cape. We hadn't rehearsed that part, but I thought it added a lot to the moment. I chanted:

"Something live, something furry,
Appear now, in a hurry!"

"Zengawii!" Frankie shouted as he pulled the cape off the hat. People in the audience moved to the edge of their seats. Everyone was completely quiet. Frankie reached into the hat. Suddenly there was a sound! It was the growl of one very angry little dog. Frankie pulled his hand out of the hat really fast. Cheerio stuck his face out, his paws hanging over the

brim of the hat. He looked at the audience. I don't
think he'd ever seen so many people in one place.

The audience burst into laughter and applause,
which must have really scared Cheerio, because he
dived back into the bottom of the hat and started
to spin. And I don't mean just normal spinning.
No, this was mega-spinning. He was going so fast
that the hat started to move down a lane.

"Is this part of the trick?" I whispered to Frankie.

"He's your dog, Zip. Don't ask me," he answered.

By that time, the hat was rocketing down the lane. It turned round and round, picking up speed

from the oil on the wood. In no time, it was at the end of the lane. *Smack!* The hat crashed into the pins, sending them flying in every direction. Nine pins went down. The last one teetered back and forth, back and forth. Almost … yes … no … yes … finally, it fell.

The crowd gasped.

"How about that for a strike!" Papa Pete yelled.

The place went wild. Everyone was applauding – everyone but Nick McKelty. He just stood by the sandwiches, scowling.

"Hey, doesn't anyone want to see my world-famous left-handed trick shot?" he yelled.

"Give it up, Nick!" I said to him. "You can't top the hat!"

He was so mad, his face turned bright red.

"Fine," he said. "Then I'm getting a Vanilla Coke. And you can't have one!"

"Is he the comeback king or what?" Ashley said. We all laughed as he stomped off.

Cheerio was out of the hat by now, sliding down the lane as he tried to make his way towards me. He looked like he was on ice skates. I think he was still feeling dizzy, because his eyes were spinning in opposite directions. I scooped him up and gave him a big hug.

I turned round. All the people in the bowling alley were on their feet cheering – for Cheerio and for us, the Magik 3.

Frankie, Ashley, Robert and I joined hands and took a bow. It was the greatest feeling of my entire life.

CHAPTER 20

There's a little balcony off our living room. It's my favourite place because at night you can see the moon from there. As I sat on the balcony and looked up at the moon, I thought about how great it feels to actually do something right.

Papa Pete slid the door open and brought out two pickles – my favourite bedtime snack. Mine was an old dill and his was a crunchy garlic. He sat down next to me and said, "You should be very proud of yourself tonight, Hank."

"I really am," I said.

We were quiet for a while, just sitting there, enjoying our pickles.

"They want to test me," I said finally.

"In what, maths?" Papa Pete asked.

"A teacher came over to our house. He said I might have learning difficulties. He said my brain might be different."

"We're all different," said Papa Pete. "That's what makes us great."

"But what if the test shows that I'm stupid?"

"Grandson of mine, there is nothing stupid about you. Didn't you build that project for school? Didn't you figure out how to make the hat work? Didn't you amaze every one of my friends tonight at the bowling alley? You're a winner, Hank."

"But I'm different."

"Take pickles," said Papa Pete. "There are big ones and little ones, smooth ones and bumpy ones, very crunchy ones and not-so-crunchy ones. There are bread-and-butter pickles, gherkins, hamburger slices, half-dills, full-dills..."

"OK, Papa Pete, I get the picture."

"The point is this," he said. "They're all different and they're all delicious to someone. And you, my grandson, are positively delicious."

I looked down at the little bit of pickle I had left. I popped it into my mouth. It was really good.

Then I looked at Papa Pete. He really knows a lot about everything. I sure hope he's right about me!

*This book is dedicated to Hank's godfather,
Alan Berger, who had the bright idea to
introduce us – H.W. and L.O.*

HANK ZIPZER

The WORLD'S GREATEST UNDERACHIEVER and the CRUNCHY PICKLE DISASTER

CHAPTER 1

"Hank, will you please stop bouncing around like a jumping bean and concentrate?" my mum asked.

"This is what I do when I concentrate," I answered.

I was hopping over to a sock that was lying on the floor of my room. When I reached the sock, I picked it up with my toes. That's a trick I learned from one of my best friends Ashley Wong. Ashley can pick up almost anything with her toes, including marbles. She can also tie a cherry stem into a knot using only her tongue. Those are qualities you want in a best friend.

I curled my toes around the sock until I had it

in my grasp. Then I swung my leg around to the side so it was sticking straight out from my body. That's a trick I learned from my other best friend Frankie Townsend. His mum is a yoga teacher, and she taught him how to twist his legs around like a pretzel. Frankie has got so good at it that he can bring his big toe all the way up to his nose – which is also an excellent way to see if your feet smell. I've never thought about this before, but my friends and I all have very talented toes. Maybe that's why we're friends.

When my leg was in the right position, I released the sock from my toe grasp and flicked it into the air towards my dirty laundry basket. It was an excellent flick, if I do say so myself. The sock sailed into the basket and landed dead centre on my boxers.

"He shoots, he scores!" I yelled, doing my wiggly victory dance.

My mum shook her head. "I came in

here to help you study your spelling words," she said with a sigh. "But frankly, Hank, I have better things to do with my time than watch you play toe basketball."

We had been studying for a while and my mum sounded like she was getting a little tetchy. I sat down on my desk chair and got serious.

"Hit me with the next word," I said to her. "I'm ready for it."

"'Receive'," said my mum. "Think before you answer, Hank. It's a tricky one."

I looked across the room, trying to see the word in my head. But instead, all I saw was my other sock, lying on the floor next to the laundry basket. I tried not to go for it, but I couldn't resist. I scooted across the room on my chair, doing a 360 degree spin at the halfway point. I don't know who invented chairs with wheels, but whoever the guy was, he was a genius.

"I thought you were going to focus, Hank," my mum said, grabbing on to the back of my chair and bringing me to a screeching stop.

"Believe it or not, I'm trying to."

She didn't like that answer. She shot me one of those Mum looks that says *Don't try to fool me, young man; I see what you're up to.* I bet you've probably seen that look before.

"I'm serious," I tried to explain to her. "I have this theory that if I keep moving, then my brain won't stop and I won't forget my spelling words. I bet it works. 'Receive' is the word, right?"

She nodded.

"OK," I said. "Receive. *R*, right?"

She started to answer, but I put my hand up to stop her. "Don't tell me. Don't tell me. OK. *Receive.* R-E-C-I-E-V-E. See? Didn't I tell you it works?"

"Hank, I hate to tell you this, but you reversed two letters."

"OK, OK. Don't tell me what they are," I said. "*Receive.* OK." I took my time and thought really hard as I spelled out the letters. "R-E-C-E-I-V-E."

"That's great," my mum said. "You got it!"

I gave her a high five. It felt good to be right.

166

"You have just seen my new Hank Zipzer guaranteed method for getting one hundred per cent," I said. "I'm going to win the spelling contest tomorrow, Mum. I am Spelling Man, Ruler of the Alphabet."

"Not so fast, Spelling Man." My mum laughed. "There's one more word left on your list."

One word? Piece of cake. I had already learned fourteen. Fourteen words neatly packed away in my brain for tomorrow's contest. It had taken most of the night, but it would be worth it just to see the look on Ms Adolf's face when I won.

Ms Adolf, my fourth-grade teacher, was going to be amazed. Hey, *I* was amazed. Never before in my whole life had I ever known how to spell all – I mean *all* – my words correctly. Spelling is one of the hardest things on the face of the earth for me. I study. I go over and over and over my spelling words. At the time, they seem to stick in my memory. They seem to be happy in my brain. But then later, like the next morning when I really need them, they seem to have orbited off into space somewhere. Or if not space, then wherever lost spelling words go. It's like they slip off the edge of my brain.

But this time I felt different. Tonight I was the master. I was the king of the country of Spelling.

I flung myself on to the bottom bunk of my bed and bounced around. "What's the last word?" I asked my mum.

"Rhythm," she said.

That was a tough one. I knew it had a lot of letters you couldn't hear, but exactly what they were was a total mystery to me. I flipped myself over and hung off the edge of the bed. All the blood flowed into my head and I wondered if a person's face could explode from doing that.

"Hank?" I could hear my mum asking. She sounded like she was far away. It was really loud inside my head, with all that blood beating like a drum. I poked around under my bed. There was a lot of interesting stuff there: a stuffed Tasmanian Devil I had won at my school fair, a plastic golf club, a pencil sharpener in the shape of the Empire State Building and a ball of dust the size of a fist.

Suddenly the ball of dust moved and from behind it, two beady eyes stared out at me. The eyes moved! Then a long, snakelike tongue shot out at me with the speed of a bullet. I flew off the bed like a rocket.

"Emily!" I screamed. "Get your creepy reptile out of here!"

My sister, Emily, is so weird that she has an iguana for a pet. How many eight-year-old girls do you know who sleep with a large, scaly lizard in their bed at night? Why can't she have a teddy bear like everyone else's little sister?

Emily came racing in. She was wearing my Mets sweatshirt, which she can do because we're about the same size. Even though she's fifteen months younger than I am, she's a little tall for her age and I'm a little short for mine.

"Emily, that's my sweatshirt," I said. "Give it back."

"Why should I?"

"You don't even like baseball," I said. "You're just trying to make me cross."

"Will you stop yelling, Hank," she said. "You're scaring Katherine."

"You got it backwards, backwad," I said. "Katherine just scared me."

Emily bent down and coaxed Katherine out from under the bed. "Come on, girl," she said, in her iguana-talking voice. "Come to your mummy lizard." Could she be any weirder?

The ball of dust had attached itself to Katherine's face and was hanging off where her lips would be if iguanas had lips. She looked like a scaly Father Christmas with a mutant beard.

"How is a guy supposed to study his spelling words with that lizard hanging out under his bed?" I asked.

"Since when do you study spelling?" Emily answered, putting Katherine on her shoulder.

"Since tonight," I said. "We're having a spelling contest tomorrow, and Ms Adolf has promised that the winner gets an *A* in spelling on his school report. That's going to be me."

"I only see one problem," said Emily. "You can't spell. Remember?"

"Watch and learn," I said with my most confident voice. I turned to my mum. "Rhythm. That's the word, right?"

"That's the one," my mum said.

I opened my mouth to spell the word. I noticed that nothing was coming out. Suddenly, I felt a little nauseous. I knew that the word was there in my mind, but I was worried that if I tried to get it, it would loosen up and float away.

Six eyes stared at me, waiting. My mum's blue ones, encouraging me to give it a try. Emily's blue ones, expecting me to get it wrong. Katherine's beady ones, giving up no clue as to what goes on inside an iguana's head. *Here goes nothing*, I thought.

"R-H-Y-T—" I stopped. *Come on, Hank*. I started again.

"R-H-Y-T-H-U-M," I said.

"Wrong," said Emily, as happy as a clam. "It's R-H-Y-T-H-M. There's no *U* – as in *U* can't spell."

"Maybe I can't spell," I said, "but at least I don't

have iguana poo on my shoulder."

Emily looked at her shoulder, and sure enough, Katherine had left a little pool of poo there for Emily to enjoy. I laughed.

"I wouldn't laugh if I were you," she said. "Remember whose sweatshirt this is."

"I'm warning you! You'd better wash it at least a hundred times." I started for her, lizard and all, but Mum stopped me.

"That's enough, you two," she said. "Emily, take your iguana back to your room. Hank, why don't you and Dad go over the words one more time. I'm going to have a bath."

Trust me, if there's one person you don't want to study your spelling words with, it's my dad. He's a crossword-puzzle nut, and he knows how to spell every word in every language and their abbreviations. And on top of that, he can't even begin to understand why spelling is hard for me.

"Just sit your butt down in your chair and study," he says all the time. "If you study, spelling is a can't-lose situation."

So I walked out of my room and sat my backside down on a chair in the living room. My dad was in his favourite chair, watching a TV talk show where a load of grown-ups talk all at once. And they say kids have bad manners. His glasses were up on top of his head, which is where he puts them when he's not reading or doing a crossword puzzle. He always forgets they're up there. Lots of times, he walks around, looking for his glasses, and we have to tell him they're on top of his head. He needs glasses to find his glasses.

"Do you want me to test you?" my dad asked.

Should I impress him? Should I try one word? *No.* I decided to just let the words rest up in my head so they would come flying out of my mouth when I needed them in class.

"Thanks, Dad, but I've studied enough. I think I'll just get a good night's sleep."

I kissed him goodnight. I always kiss him on the left cheek. It's dangerous to kiss him on the right one – you could get poked with a pencil. My dad keeps a pencil tucked behind his right ear. He keeps it there in case he suddenly remembers a word he's been trying to think of. If you're as much of a crossword maniac as my dad is, you don't want to let something as important as a four-letter word for nostril get away from you.

I went into the bathroom to get ready for bed. As I brushed my teeth, I let myself imagine what it would feel like to win the spelling contest. Ms Adolf would smile at me for the first time ever. I closed my eyes and saw her handing me an *A*. Not a paper one either – a solid gold one, like the statues that movie stars get at the Oscars. My gold *A* would be so heavy that I'd have trouble carrying it back to my seat. I'd put it up on my desk so that everyone in my class or passing by our door could see it. Every kid in the class would congratulate me, even the class bully, Nick "The Tick" McKelty. Oh yeah, he'd smile at me with his big wonky teeth and say, "I wish that was mine." That would be sweet.

I opened my eyes, looked into the mirror and imagined my classmates slapping me on the back. I smiled. My teeth were blue from my gel toothpaste.

"Thank you very much. Yes, I am very proud of myself. Very, very proud."

As I said the word "proud", a big wad of toothpaste flew out of my mouth and splattered all over the bathroom mirror. I started to wipe it off with my Mets flannel. I looked around to see if anyone was watching and then scooped a little of the gel on to my finger. I used it to write on the mirror.

"R-H-Y-T-H-M," I wrote in sparkly blue letters. I stepped back and stared at the word. For once, it was spelled correctly. I did my wiggly victory dance.

I could hardly wait for the next day. I was going to get my first *A*.

CHAPTER 2

I must have slept through my alarm, because the next morning I woke up ten minutes later than usual. The last thing I wanted was to be late for school – or "tardy", as Ms Adolf says. Ms Adolf told us that tardy pupils don't get to participate in spelling contests. If you're even thirty seconds late to class, she writes a big, red *T* next to your name in her register. She once sent Ryan Shimozato to Head Teacher Love's office for having two *T*s in a row, even though he had a sprained ankle from football and had to walk with crutches. I don't know if Ms Adolf is the meanest fourth-grade teacher that ever lived, but she's in the top three, for sure.

I threw on some clothes, grabbed a waffle from the toaster and flew out of the door and into the lift. I wished I'd had the time to soak the waffle in syrup, but I knew Ashley and Frankie were already waiting for me in front of our building. Frankie lives on the sixth floor and Ashley lives on the fourth. It's so great to have your best friends live in the same building. We don't have to schedule playdates like lots of other kids in our class. Whenever we want to get together, we just pick up the phone and say, "Meet me in the basement." That's where we have our clubhouse, which is also the World Headquarters for Magik 3, our magic act.

Frankie is an amazing magician. Ashley and I are his assistants. Magik 3 has performed in public twice. The first time, at my grandpa's bowling league party, we were a smash hit. The second time was at Tyler King's fourth birthday party. His family lives across the hall from me. His mum had heard how good we were at the bowling party and offered us fifteen dollars to do a magic show at Tyler's party. For our opening, Frankie said his special magic word, which is *"Zengawii"*, and made a quarter appear out of Tyler's ear. The problem was Tyler said he wanted a million more quarters. When Frankie tried to explain that he didn't have a million quarters, Tyler went bonkers and said he hated the *Zengawii* man and wanted him to go back to his magic castle and never come back. He's still saying that to everyone he sees, so we're waiting until he calms down before we hand out our business cards in the building.

Frankie and Ashley were outside, hopping up and down to keep their feet warm. I shivered when I hit the cold air. It was the first week in November, and I could feel the New York winter just around the corner.

Unlike myself, Frankie and Ashley were dressed for the weather. Ashley was wearing a purple parka with a matching purple hat that she had decorated with rhinestones. She glues rhinestones on to all her clothes – even her shoes and the frames of her glasses. That's Ashley for you. Frankie had on a Yankees coat.

"Did you have to wear that?" I asked him, like the loyal Mets fan that I am.

"Yes, I did, Zip," he said, "because I dress like a winner."

"Fine, then I'll let you borrow my Mets sweatshirt."

"The Mets? Those losers?"

"Our day will come," I shot back. "Mets fans are patient."

"You two have to stop this right now or we'll never get to school," said Ashley, who isn't a baseball fan at all. Believe it or not, she watches professional table tennis.

I don't know how much you know about baseball, so let me just tell you this right now. If you live in New York and like baseball, you're either a Mets fan or a Yankees fan. You can't be both. Mets fans like the underdog, the team that comes from behind. Yankees fans go for the easy win. But that's just my opinion. It says a lot about my friendship with Frankie that we can be such good friends even though we're on different sides of the fence, baseball-wise.

"Hank, you're going to be cold," said Frankie's father, Dr Townsend, who was walking us to school. Dr Townsend isn't the kind of doctor you go to when you have a sore throat. He's a doctor of African-American studies, which is what he teaches at Columbia University. "Where's your coat?"

"Oops," I said. "I'll be right back."

My father always says, "What you don't have in your mind you have in your feet," meaning I had to go all the way back upstairs to get my coat. There was no time to wait for the lift, so I ran up the ten flights to our flat. I dashed inside and reached for my coat, but it wasn't in the cupboard where I had left it – or at least, where I *thought* I had left it.

"Mum, have you seen my green coat?" I shouted. I was breathing hard from the run upstairs.

My dad came out of the bedroom in his T-shirt and boxer shorts, which is not really something you want to see first thing in the morning. Actually, it's not something you want to see at any time of the day.

"Your mother's already left," he said. "She had to take Emily to a dental appointment."

Now, ordinarily, I would've asked something like, "Why, were her fangs bothering her?" But Frankie is always telling me about good karma. He got that from his mum, who is a big believer in karma. Basically, karma means that if you put out something good, you get something good back. If you put out something rotten, it comes back and bites you in the bum.

Since I really, really wanted to win the spelling contest, I figured this was no day to take any chances with my karma, so I decided to hold off on the fangs remark.

Instead, I said to my dad, "Poor Emily. I hope the dentist doesn't do anything that's going to hurt her." Boy, if that didn't guarantee me some excellent karma, I didn't know what would.

My dad was looking around for my coat, grumbling about how I never put anything where it belongs.

"There it is," I said, pointing to our dachshund, Cheerio. Cheerio was lying on the sofa, looking so cute all curled up on my coat. I gently pulled it out from under him.

"Don't go nuts on me, boy," I whispered. "I'm in a hurry."

Cheerio went nuts anyway. He jumped off the sofa and started to spin round in a circle. When he does that, which is fairly often, he looks like a big, furry cheerio, which is how he got his name. Our vet says his spinning thing is a reaction to stress. I don't know what he's got to be stressed about. I mean, all he has to do is eat and pee. No one's asking him to spell *receive* or *rhythm*.

I put on my coat and ran downstairs. Frankie was looking at his watch. "We thought maybe you went upstairs and went back to bed, didn't we, Ashweena?" he said. Frankie has nicknames for everyone. He calls his dad "Double *T*", because his name is Thomas Townsend. "We better get a move on. We don't want to be tardy, do we?" Ashley

183

asked, doing a pretty good imitation of Ms Adolf.

It's two blocks from our building to our school. We had to walk really fast to get to there on time. Luckily, we arrived just before the bell rang. We said goodbye to Dr Townsend, raced upstairs and slid into our seats just as Ms Adolf was closing our classroom door.

Ms Adolf was wearing a grey skirt and blouse, just like she had worn the day before and the day before that and every day since school started. I guess she figures grey looks good on her because it matches her grey face. You should see her hairdo. It looks like she has a stack of hairy grey doughnuts piled up on top of her head. I'm sorry if this grosses you out, but I have to tell it like I see it.

The other teachers on our floor still had their Halloween decorations up, but not our class. In fact, Ms Adolf had never put any up in the first place. She thinks Halloween is a silly occasion, because all you do is dress up and eat sweets and have fun. I bet her favourite holiday to celebrate is the Day of the Dead.

Instead of ghosts and goblins and pumpkins, the walls of our class are decorated with artwork from our states project. We each picked a US state and outlined it in the colour of the product it's most famous for. For example, Florida is orange because of its orange groves and Vermont is brown because of its maple syrup. I picked Rhode Island because I like the shape of it. I outlined it in red for the red hen, which is the state bird. Rhode Island is the smallest state and its motto is "Hope". If people had mottos, I think I'd pick "hope" for mine. I really do hope a lot. In fact, I was hoping that I would win the spelling contest that morning.

"Now, pupils, today is our spelling contest," Ms Adolf said, "and we're all going to have great fun. I know *I* am."

Call me crazy, but I don't know how anyone can think spelling is even *slightly* fun, let alone *great* fun. Rollercoasters are fun. Riding bikes in the park is fun. Baseball games are fun. But spelling is definitely not fun, unless you're the type of person who enjoys having injections at the doctor's. Then you'd probably think spelling is a barrel of laughs.

"Here are the rules," said Ms Adolf. "Pupils will be asked to spell fifteen words, the ones I assigned to each of you at the beginning of the week. Those pupils who get all the words on their list correct may participate in the final round, which covers all the words on all lists. As soon as you miss a word in that round, you must sit down. The last pupil standing will be the winner and will receive an *A* on his or her school report. Are there any questions?"

Luke Whitman put his hand up.

"Can I go to the nurse's office and lie down?" he asked. "I feel sick." Luke Whitman asks if he can go to the nurse's office every single day and Ms Adolf's answer is always the same.

"Absolutely not," said Ms Adolf. "Now, who wants to go first in today's spelling contest?"

Nick McKelty put his thick arm in the air and waved it around like he had a gigantic toilet emergency.

"I'll go first!" he grunted. "I am totally, two hundred per cent prepared."

He always says things like that. He claims his parents are best friends with the mayor of New York or he tells you he got the highest maths score ever recorded in the Western hemisphere. We call it

The McKelty Factor – truth times a hundred.

Even though Nick the Tick was acting like a total nerd, secretly I was glad he put his hand up. At least it meant that Ms Adolf wasn't going to pick me. Usually she picks me first. I think it makes her happy when I don't have the right answer, no matter what the subject.

As McKelty got up to go to the front of the classroom, he walked close enough to me that I got a mega-whiff of his bad, bad breath. He must have eaten an entire raw onion for breakfast because his breath smelled like a rhinoceros with tooth decay. Not that I know what a rhinoceros with tooth decay smells like, but I bet it's pretty foul.

you try holding a toothbrush with these feet!

"Hey, girls," McKelty said to Frankie and me as he walked by. "Ready to see a spelling master at work?"

"Sure, Nick," Frankie whispered. "Who you got in mind?"

I laughed and Ms Adolf shot me a wicked look.

"Since you seem to find this so funny, Henry, you'll go next," she said.

I wish she'd call me Hank. No one calls me Henry, except my mum when she's really angry and Paula, the woman who makes appointments at my dentist's surgery. No one but Ms Adolf, that is. I've told her a million times that all my friends call me Hank. She says she sees no need for that, because my real name is Henry. Besides, she's not my friend.

My heart started to beat faster. I looked over at Frankie, who gave me his famous smile, the one we call The Big Dimple. He says a lot with that smile. This time, it said, *You can do it, Zip. Just breathe*.

Frankie must tell me to breathe four times a day. As a matter of fact, he tells everyone to breathe if he thinks they are getting too tense about things.

Ms Adolf gave Nick fifteen words to spell. As usual, he was all talk and no walk. Out of the fifteen words, he spelled seven right and missed eight. No *A* for him, that millipede.

All during his turn, I tried to review my words. My brain was swimming in letters. They were all over the place but were not making themselves into any words I knew. *Breathe*, I said to myself. *You can do this, Hank. Piece of cake.* I tried really hard to talk myself into believing my own words. But in my brain, right underneath those words, were the other more familiar words: *no way, Hank.*

Ms Adolf must have called my name, but I was concentrating so hard, I didn't hear her at first. All of a sudden, I saw her standing over me. The entire class was staring at me. Every eye was burning into my skin.

"Daydreaming, are we?" Ms Adolf asked.

"No," I answered. "Just practising my words. I guess I can't spell and hear at the same time."

The kids cracked up, and I had to smile. There it was, the old Zipzer attitude. I still had it. I hadn't meant to be funny, but the sound of the kids enjoying my answer did feel good.

The feeling didn't last, however.

"Come with me, young man," Ms Adolf commanded. I walked up to the front of the room and turned towards the class.

As I looked out at all the faces, my ears stopped working for real. It was as if everything was moving in slow motion. I looked over at Ms Adolf and saw her lips move, but I couldn't hear a thing.

Ms Adolf repeated the word "rhythm". I read her lips. *Come on, Hank, breathe. You know this word.*

My body started working again.

"Rhythm," I said. "R-H-Y-T-H-M, rhythm." Without realizing it, I high-fived myself. The class laughed again.

"Quiet! This is not a laughing matter," Ms Adolf reminded them. "All right, Mr Comedian. Try 'receive'."

"R-E-C..." I paused. So far, so good. Then my mind went totally blank.

R-E-C-what? I know there's an E *and an* I, *but which comes first? What's the rule? I before* E *except after* – *Oh no, what's the word? I forgot the word. What word was I spelling? How can I be so stupid? Breathe… I am breathing. I'm just not remembering.*

"Well, Henry, there is more to the word receive than R-E-C," Ms Adolf said.

Oh yeah, thank goodness – receive!

"I know this; don't tell me," I blurted out with confidence.

"Oh, trust me, I won't," Ms Adolf assured me.

"R-E-C-I-E-V-E, receive." *Oh please, oh please, let that be right.*

"I thought you said you knew it," she said. "I'll give you one more chance. Try 'neighbour'."

"Neighbour," I said. "N-A…"

Where did it go?

Last night I knew every one of these words forwards and backwards. This morning, I'd lost them. From the time I left my flat to the time I arrived in class, they must've fallen out of my head. Maybe I lost them on the street or in the hallway or the stairwell coming up to the classroom.

I started to hit my forehead. Maybe I could shake them loose from their hiding place in my brain. *How can this be happening?*

"What are you doing, Henry?" asked Ms Adolf.

"I'm trying to wake my brain up. Maybe the words are holding on to the sides of my brain and won't fall down into my mouth." The class laughed again, but this time I really wasn't being funny.

"Try 'separate'," Ms Adolf said.

"Do I have to?"

"Try 'separate' now."

"I know it starts with an *S*."

"Sit down, Henry."

"But, Ms Adolf, I studied these words. I know this."

"I'm going to count to three, Henry. If you're not in your seat when I say three, you're going to the head teacher's office."

"Ms Adolf, you believe in second chances, don't you? I'm sure you do." I was begging.

"One…"

"Just give me another minute. It takes a while for

my brain to fire up. I'm like an old car – I just have to give it a little petrol."

"Two…"

"Please don't say three, Ms Adolf. Just let me try one more word, because I'm feeling like I can…"

"Three."

She said it. She said three.

I can't believe she said three.

CHAPTER 4

As I walked down the stairs to Mr Love's office, I felt like I had taken that walk a hundred times before. I felt that way because I had.

Mr Love and I have spent a whole lot of time together, having long talks. And I don't mean the "How about those Mets?" kind of talks, either. Nope, the kind of talks I have with Mr Love are listening to him tell me what I've done wrong, and according to him, that's pretty much everything.

I don't know how this happens. I try to behave in school. I'm not like Nick McKelty, who gets a kick out of being an idiot. And I'm certainly not like Luke Whitman, whose full-time job is getting into trouble. I try to follow the rules. I try hard, but somehow I always end up doing face time with Head Teacher Love.

For example, take the first day of fourth grade: Ms Adolf said we had to write a five-paragraph essay describing what we did during our summer holidays. It's really hard for me to write a five-paragraph essay, so I decided to create a living essay. Instead of writing about our visit to Niagara Falls, I made a model of Niagara Falls out of papier-mâché. I even attached it to the sink in our class so that real water could run through it. Was it my fault that the water overflowed and gushed all over the floor? Was it my fault that Ms Adolf got blasted in the face by the water hose? Was it my fault that Mr Love stepped on a floating lunch bag and a tuna sandwich exploded in his face?

I reached the first floor and walked towards

the office. Mrs Crock was in the attendance office and looked up when she saw me.

"Oh no, Hank." She sighed. "Not again."

"Mrs Crock," I said, "would you like to hear me spell 'separate'?"

"Why, yes, dear, if you'd like me to," she answered.

"S-E-P-A-R-A-T-E," I said.

"That's very lovely spelling, dear," she said. "Have a seat on the bench and I'll page Head Teacher Love. He's in the dining room."

I sat down on the bench in the hall. *Separate. There it was, just waiting on the tip of my tongue. I knew it was there all along. If only Ms Adolf had given me another chance.*

I heard footsteps approaching, but I knew it wasn't Mr Love. He always wears rubber-soled Velcro shoes that make a squeaking sound on the lino when he walks. These footsteps were clicking, not squeaking.

"Hank? Is that you?" a man's voice asked.

I looked up. It was Mr Rock. Mr Rock is the music teacher at PS 87. I met him at the beginning of the school year, when I did a week of detention in his classroom after school. We did the coolest things, like listen to music and talk about our all-time favourite cars. I was so embarrassed that he was seeing me in the head teacher's office.

"Ms Adolf sent me to see Mr Love," I told him, before he could ask.

"What's your crime?" He asked it like he was joking around.

"I wouldn't sit down during the spelling contest."

"Forty lashes with a wet noodle for you."

He smiled. He was joking around! Mr Rock is the nicest teacher you could ever hope to meet.

Squeak, squeak, squeak. Mr Love and his dancing Velcro feet were coming down the hall. I stood up, feeling nervous. Mr Rock leaned over and whispered in my ear.

"Speak up for yourself in there, Hank," he said. "You're a great kid."

Then he gave me a high five and left.

When he saw me at his office door, Mr Love did not look happy. Neither did his mole.

Mr Love has this mole on his face that I swear looks like the Statue of Liberty without the torch.

Ashley and Frankie disagree. Ashley thinks it looks like a cherry stone. Frankie says it looks like one of those crackers that's shaped like a goldfish. But I say my opinion goes, since I've spent way more time in the head teacher's office than both Frankie and Ashley combined. I've had a lot of mole-viewing time.

"I see we meet again, Mr Zipzer," Mr Love said in his big-man voice. Even though he's not much taller than I am, Head Teacher Love has a really loud voice. He always sounds like he's on the loudspeaker system, even though he isn't.

I followed him into his office.

"Sit down, young man," he said, pointing to the chair across from his desk. "You're spending so much time here, I believe that seat is starting to take the shape of your rear end."

I laughed. He didn't.

"I'll let you know when something funny happens," he said. "Until then, keep your laughter to yourself."

He read over the note Ms Adolf had sent with me, rubbing his chin as he read. He was dangerously close to touching his mole. I wonder if when he touches it, he screams, "Ugh!" I know I would.

"I read here that Ms Adolf asked you to sit down and you did not," he said.

I cleared my throat and tried to speak. Something came out, but it wasn't words. It was mostly air, with a croaking froggy sound mixed in. Mr Love makes you nervous, even if you're trying not to be nervous.

"Speak up, young man," he said.

I tried again, and a few words came out this time. "I hadn't finished spelling, sir."

"But your directions were to sit down," he said. "Were they not?"

I didn't answer, because everyone at PS 87 knows that when Leland Love asks a question, he likes to answer it himself.

"Yes, they were," he said, proving my point. "I'm going to tell you something, Mr Zipzer," he continued, "and I want you to carry this thought with you for the rest of your school years. It may be the best single piece of advice you ever get."

Wow. I was ready for that. I slid forward to the edge of my chair. *Lay it on me*, I thought.

Mr Love cleared his throat.

"Following directions will get you where you need to be, no matter where you are," he said.

If that is the best piece of advice I'll ever get, I hope I never hear the worst.

"It just so happens that you have caught me in a very good mood," said Mr Love, "and so I'm going to let you off with a warning." He reached down and loosened one of the Velcro straps on his shoes. "Do you know why I'm in a good mood, Mr Zipzer?"

"Because you really, really love your Velcro shoes?" I asked.

"That's one reason," he said. "They are so convenient. But the second reason is that today is fish day in the dining room, and I am about to go and enjoy a fine piece of halibut. Just for the halibut, that is."

He threw his head back and laughed so loudly it gave me the creeps. "Something funny just happened," he said. "You may laugh now, Mr Zipzer."

He laughed again, and the Statue of Liberty mole wiggled back and forth as if it was doing the hula. *It must like fish too,* I thought.

CHAPTER 5

The only decent thing about the spelling contest was that Ashley won. She is such a good friend that her winning almost made up for the fact that my spelling was a total disaster.

"Cheer up, Zip," Frankie said to me, as we sat down at our table in the dining room. "So, you're not a speller. Big deal."

"I'm also not an adder or a subtracter or a reader or a writer," I said. "Let's face it, Frankie. I'm a school flop."

I was feeling pretty terrible. First, I messed up the spelling contest, for no good reason that I could see. Then I got sent to the head teacher's office.

And if those things hadn't made the day horrible enough, the halibut made the entire dining room smell like toxic waste.

"There's more to life than school," said Frankie, pulling out his peanut-butter-and-jam sandwich. "Don't be so hard on yourself."

That's easy for Frankie to say. He's one of those kids who's good at everything. He reads like a grown-up – even the newspaper. He actually *reads* the sports section every day. Not me. I have to watch ESPN for my updates. He's also really funny, a phenomenal magician, and all the girls like him too.

"What's up, Frankie?" asked Katie Sperling and Kim Paulson as they walked by with their trays.

See what I mean? The two most beautiful girls in the fourth grade weren't asking, "What's up, Hank?"

My father always says that Frankie Townsend is going to be the president of the United States one day. Of course, he also says that Emily is going to be a rocket scientist, as though that's ever going to happen. I can see it now: Emily cruising around

Mission Control with Katherine – flashing her sticky tongue out at all the astronauts – on her shoulder. *Houston, we have a problem. We have an ugly iguana loose on the launchpad with its tongue stuck to the windscreen.*

I pulled out my sandwich. My mum had packed me another one of her science experiments. Inside the bag with my sandwich was a note from her.

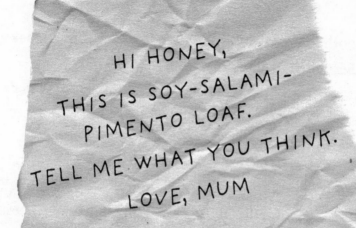

HI HONEY,
THIS IS SOY-SALAMI-
PIMENTO LOAF.
TELL ME WHAT YOU THINK.
LOVE, MUM

My mum runs a deli called The Crunchy Pickle, which my grandfather Papa Pete started. When she took over the deli, my mum said she wanted to bring lunch meats into the world of healthy eating. So she's always inventing stuff like soy-salami-pimento loaf. I'm her number-one guinea pig.

"That stuff looks nasty," Frankie said, giving my sandwich the evil eye. "Here, mate. Have half of mine. Yours looks like it has a rash, with all those red spots."

The peanut-butter-and-jam sandwich tasted great. It was the first good thing that had happened to me that day.

Ashley arrived with her tray. Her parents are

both doctors. They don't usually have time to make her lunch in the mornings.

"Robert alert," she said, shaking her chocolate milk. "Sorry, guys. I couldn't ditch him. He's on me like glue."

Robert Upchurch was following Ashley to our table. He lives in our building, and even though he's only in the third grade, he thinks he's best friends with us. We don't have the heart to tell him he's not. I mean, the kid wears a tie to school every day. He's already got a hard enough life, right?

Robert took a seat next to me.

"Greetings," he said, which is a typical Robert thing to say. He talks like he's an alien in a movie. They're always saying stuff like, "I bring you greetings from my people."

A horrible smell drifted up into my nose. It was coming from Robert's tray. I couldn't believe it. He'd actually got the halibut – school dinner fish, the lowest of the low.

"Robert, I can't believe you got the fish," I said. "I've never seen *anyone* get the fish."

"Actually, fish is excellent for the brain," Robert said. "It's full of fatty oils that provide nutrients, which the brain needs to function. Maybe that's why I'm so intelligent."

"Or maybe that's why you smell so bad," said Frankie, holding his nose.

Robert laughed. You have to give him credit for that. You can say almost anything to him and he doesn't take offence.

"How was the spelling contest?" he asked, chomping down on a mouthful of fish.

"Can we talk about something else?" I asked.

"Sure," said Robert. "Would you like to talk about penguins? I know a great deal about the king penguin. It weighs up to forty pounds and grows to be three feet tall."

Without taking a breath, Robert launched into the life cycle of the penguin. It was like having a *National Geographic* special right there at the lunch table.

Suddenly, I smelled something *really* foul behind me. Immediately, I realized it was the unmistakable odour of a rhinoceros with tooth decay – Nick McKelty breath.

"Nice work today on the spelling, dodo brain," McKelty said, leaning over my shoulder to grab the last of my jam doughnut.

"You didn't exactly light up the room yourself, McKelty," I said.

"I just didn't want to make you stupid ones feel bad," McKelty said. "I knew every word."

"Right," said Frankie. "And my name is Bernice."

From the next table, Katie and Kim cracked up. Everyone loves it when Frankie does his "Bernice" line. Everyone but McKelty, that is. Bullies don't like to be laughed at. He pulled himself up to his full height and, I have to admit, he towered over Frankie.

"Listen, Townsend, you say that one more time and I'm going have my father call your father," he said. Nick's father owns McKelty's Roll 'N Bowl, the bowling alley where my grandpa plays.

"And what's he going to say?" I asked. "Lane number three is available?"

Now Ryan Shimozato and his crew started to laugh. Luke Whitman cracked up too, but not too loudly.

"Bowling shoes make your feet stink," he said. That's typical Luke Whitman. Luke is one of those kids who'll say disgusting things like "booger slime" or "toe jam" or "diaper doo-doo" for no reason at all. I'll bet there's a kid like that in your class.

McKelty was really mad now. He was searching for a comeback, but the big lug just couldn't come up with anything.

"Frankie," said Ashley, "can you make Mr McKelty here disappear?"

"No problemo," said Frankie.

He stood up and looked over at Kim and Katie. He flashed them The Big Dimple. Boy, were they going for it too. But this is what is so cool about Frankie Townsend. He could've done the magic all by himself and got all that attention from Katie and Kim for himself. But did he? No. Here's what he did. He took me by the arm and pulled me to my feet.

"I can't do magic without my man here. Zip, give me some of your magical moves, mate."

Kim and Katie stared at me. In fact, everyone in the dining room stopped what they were doing and looked at me. Frankie gave me the nod and I started to wave my hands around like I was casting a spell. Frankie and I have watched *Behind the*

Scenes: Secrets of Magic videos until the tapes were practically worn out, so I have the moves down pretty smoothly. I gave it the full show-business treatment. Frankie let me go on until he saw that Katie and Kim were impressed. Then he stood up and closed his eyes. When he spoke, it was almost a whisper.

"Bones of halibut, magic thing,
Sound the bell! Zengawii! Ring!"

He opened his eyes, and the very second he did, the bell rang. I'm not kidding. It was amazing.

"Lunch is over; everyone back to class," said Mrs Tomasini, the teacher on lunch duty. "Nick McKelty, that means you. Get going right now. Quickly."

Nick picked up his rucksack and hurried out of the dining room.

"Wow," Katie said to Frankie. "You *did* make him disappear."

"You guys are great!" said Kim, smiling at me. "Can I walk back to class with you?"

"Why not," I answered, giving her my big smile. I may be dumb in spelling, but hey, I'm no dummy.

CHAPTER 6

I spent most of the afternoon smiling at Kim Paulson. She sits in front of me, so I was actually smiling at the back of her head. But, trust me, the back of her head is very nice. I couldn't believe how a day that had started so terribly had turned out so good.

I was in such a fine mood that it didn't even bother me that much when Ms Adolf said she was handing out our school reports. It was just before the end of school that day. As we packed up our books, Ms Adolf went to her desk and unlocked the top drawer with a silver key that she wears round her neck. She took out her register, which was stuffed full of envelopes. Then she walked up and down the aisles, handing out the report cards individually. She gave each person a small, white envelope that was addressed to their parents.

When Ms Adolf arrived at my desk, I put my hand out to receive my white school-report envelope. But instead of handing me one of the small envelopes that everyone else had got, Ms Adolf pulled out a large, brown manila envelope.

"Your report is inside, Henry, along with a letter to your parents. Please see that they call me immediately."

Everyone sitting around me went quiet. I looked around the class. No one else had got a big brown envelope. I didn't know what it meant, but I knew way down in my stomach that it wasn't good. It took exactly one second for Nick McKelty to open his big mouth.

"Dear Mr and Mrs Zipzer," he said, making his voice sound like Ms Adolf's. "This is to inform you that your son is a stupid retardo."

A few kids laughed. I was so embarrassed that I could feel the tips of my ears turning red. I grabbed my rucksack. I had to get out of there. Fortunately, the bell rang.

"I have to go to the toilet," I said to Frankie. "I'll meet you downstairs."

I ran to the bathroom, ducked into one of the cubicles and locked the door. I think my hands were shaking as I ripped open the brown envelope. I pulled out my report and looked at it.

I'd got a *D* in spelling. But that wasn't the worst of it.

I'd also got a *D* in reading.

I'd also got a *D* in maths.

There was a note to my parents from Ms Adolf. It was written in cursive. I couldn't make out all the words, but I got a few of them. *Doesn't follow directions ... Poor study habits ... Sloppy work ... Fails to pay attention ... Below-average performance.*

It wasn't all bad news, though. I did get a *B*-plus in PE. And let's not forget music. I got a *B*-plus in music too.

I leaned my head against the door of the cubicle. I felt like I wanted to throw up.

Look on the bright side, Hank. Make yourself smile. So you'll never learn to read or write or do maths. But you're a whizz at dodgeball and you can carry a tune. Good. When you grow up, you can be a singing dodgeball player.

I tried to laugh at my own joke, but you know what? I cried instead.

CHAPTER 7

I **couldn't stay** in the toilet cubicle for ever. I wanted to, but I knew at some point I would have to leave. As I walked downstairs to meet my friends, I made a list in my head.

THE TOP TEN THINGS THAT WILL HAPPEN BECAUSE OF MY SCHOOL REPORT

(EXCEPT THERE'S ONLY SEVEN BECAUSE THAT'S ALL I COULD COME UP WITH)

BY HANK ZIPZER

1. My parents won't be able to think of a punishment big enough for me. They'll have to hire an evil punishment expert, like Darth Vader, to think of one.

2. My sister and her iguana will laugh at me for months. And I won't be able to stop them.

3. I will have to repeat the fourth grade for ever. Ms Adolf and I will grow old together, and I'll turn all grey and rinkled like her.

4. My middle name will be changed from Daniel to "Detention King".

6. Kim Paulson will never let me walk to class with her again. I don't even want to walk with me — so why would she?

7. Here's the worst: Nick McKelty will tease me about being stupid, and he'll be right.

8.

CHAPTER 8

Did you notice that I skipped number five on the list?

And that I left off the W in "wrinkled"?

It's just more proof that I deserve those lousy marks I got.

CHAPTER 9

Frankie and Ashley were waiting for me at the bottom of the stairs. They looked worried.

"Zip, are you OK?" Frankie asked. "You're not looking too good, mate."

"I'm not feeling too good, either," I said.

"Maybe you have a temperature," Ashley said, putting her hand on my forehead, the way my mum does when she thinks I have a fever.

"Don't touch me in public, Ash," I said. "I'm not that kind of sick, anyway. I got bad marks on my report."

"Like Cs?" Ashley asked.

"Ashweena, a C isn't a bad mark," Frankie

218

said. "At least, I don't think it is. Otis got one once in the fourth grade."

Otis is Frankie's older brother. He's in the eighth grade and is clever like Frankie.

"Did he get in trouble?" Ashley asked.

"Not really," Frankie said. "My dad told him a C was a warning sign that he had to work harder. 'Give it some more gas,' he said."

At our school, PS 87, we don't get letter marks until the fourth grade. Up until then, your teachers only write comments on your report, and they're usually pretty nice. In first grade, my teacher, Ms Yukelson, wrote, "Hank has excellent scissors skills and has made many valuable contributions to our unit on the harbour." My parents took me out to dinner to celebrate that report. In third grade, my teacher, Mr Chan, wrote, "Hank is a natural leader and is well liked by his peers. He needs additional practice of his reading and maths skills." We didn't go out and celebrate for that one, but it wasn't terrible, either.

"Not to worry, Zip," Frankie said, throwing his arm round my shoulder. "So what if you got a C or two on your school report? You've just got to give it a little more gas, right?"

"Pedal to the metal," said Ashley.

I had to tell them the truth. They were my best friends.

"Listen up, guys. I didn't get a C," I said. "I got three Ds. In spelling, in maths and in reading. And a really bad letter to my parents."

For a minute, Frankie and Ashley didn't say anything. Then Ashley gave me a hug and said I would do better on the next report. Frankie offered to tutor me in maths. I tell you, I have world-class friends.

Robert came to meet us for the walk home. While he was taking off his clip-on tie, which he does every day at exactly ten minutes past three, I told him the news about my report. There's no point trying to keep anything from Robert. He finds everything out sooner or later. He's like an information magnet.

"I imagine three Ds is well below the national average for fourth-graders," Robert said.

"Not now, Robert," Ashley said firmly.

He looked at me like my favourite pet goldfish had just died. Then he did a really weird thing.

He asked if he could have my Rollerblades.

"Your parents are going to ground you for so long," he said, "that by the time you get ungrounded, the Rollerblades won't even fit you any more."

"Not now, Robert," Frankie said, in the same tone Ashley had used.

I think, in his own way, Robert was trying to joke around to make me feel better. But all his joke did was bring our attention to that word: *parents*.

My parents weren't going to be happy. It's not that they're mega-strict or anything. It's just that they have expectations. And their main expectation is that my sister and I do well at school. Emily more than meets their expectations – no problem. It's me who's the dud.

I decided that the best thing to do was talk to Papa Pete, who picks us up from school three days a week. Of everyone I know, he'd be the best person to help me figure out a way to break the bad news to my parents.

Papa Pete always seems to understand me when other people don't. I told him that once, when we were sitting on my balcony and sharing a pickle, which is our favourite thing to do. He put his big, hairy arm round me and said, "Hank, my boy. That's what grandpas are for."

He is a great grandpa; there's no doubt about it. But I think it's more than that, too. Papa Pete says that everyone has a special gift in life. I think I know what his is. He's one of those people who can make you feel good no matter what. For example, once, when I was little, I stepped on a bee at the beach. It hurt so much that even after the bee sting healed, I limped around for the rest of our holiday. Everyone else in my family teased me about limping so much, but not Papa Pete. He said to me, "Hank, my boy. If I had stepped on that bee, I'd be dragging my whole leg around like a sack of potatoes." Papa Pete never makes you feel bad for what you're feeling, even if what you're feeling is silly.

We walked outside and sat on the steps, waiting for Papa Pete to show up. He was a little late, which wasn't like him. I didn't mind waiting, though. The cold air felt good.

I looked down Amsterdam Avenue. People were crowding along the street, carrying their groceries home, buying a takeaway pizza, pushing buggies, walking their kids home from school. They all seemed so happy. I wondered if any of them had ever got three Ds. That truly can suck the happiness right out of you.

"Hey, look," said Frankie. "It's Silent Stan, the crossword-puzzle man."

I looked across the street, and sure enough, my father was coming towards us.

Uh-oh, I thought, which is not what you want to be thinking when you see your father. *Maybe he has already heard about my school report.*

"Hi, Dad," I said when he reached us. "I thought Papa Pete was coming."

"He's busy," my dad answered. "He called me at home and asked me to get you kids. He's going to meet us at the deli."

He probably has a hot bowling game he can't leave, I thought. Papa Pete spends a lot of time at McKelty's Roll 'N Bowl, where he's the best senior bowler in the league. His team is called The Chopped Livers.

"Hi, kids," my father said, nodding to Frankie and Ashley. "Always good to see you, Robert."

My father really likes Robert, because Robert helps him out with his crossword puzzles. The day before, when my dad couldn't think of a three-letter word for "infection result", Robert came up with "pus". Those moments have given them a special connection.

I should explain that my dad doesn't just lie around the house all day doing crossword puzzles and waiting for calls from Papa Pete. He works at home, doing something with computers. He's tried to describe to me exactly what he does, but when he talks about computer programming, it sounds to me like he's saying, "blah, blah, blahdity, blahdity,

blah blah blahdity blahdity blah blah

blah, blah." I'm not exaggerating, either. My mind just doesn't follow what he's saying.

We started down Amsterdam Avenue, walking fast to keep up with all the people on the street. You have to do that in New York. They don't like slowcoaches here.

"So, Mr Z.," Frankie said. "Is Papa Pete OK?"

"He's fine," said my dad. "He had a garlic emergency."

We stopped at the corner of 78th Street and waited for the lights to change. My father went on talking, which was strange, because he doesn't usually say much. We leaned in closer so we could hear him over the honking. Two taxis were having a horn-blowing war.

"Vince Gristediano, who owns the biggest supermarket chain in the city, called your mother today," my dad said. "He has heard about her vegetarian lunch meats and he may want to carry her whole line of soy salami in his stores. He asked her to make samples so he can try them out on his store managers tomorrow."

"My mum shops at Gristediano's," said Ashley.

"Actually, everyone does," said Robert. "They have thirty-nine shops in Manhattan alone."

"So if Mr Gristediano buys Mum's soy salami, will we be rich?" I asked.

"I don't know about that," said my dad. "But it would definitely be a big order. It could be the start of a wonderful business for her."

"So what does this have to do with Papa Pete?" I asked.

"He's working with your mum on the salami samples for tomorrow," Dad said. "They're mixing up some new batches. Papa Pete felt the salami needed more garlic."

I smiled. Papa Pete thinks everything needs more garlic. He thinks plain garlic needs more garlic.

The lights changed, and my dad stepped out into the street.

"This is great news," I whispered to Frankie.

"Why? Because you're going to be rich?"

"No," I said. "Because with all the excitement, they'll forget to ask about my school report."

"And the problem disappears," said Frankie. He waved his hands out in front of him, like he was waving his magic wand.

"Well, it won't exactly disappear. I mean, I'll still have to figure out how to explain my marks to my parents, but at least I'll have the whole weekend to talk to Papa Pete and come up with a strategy." I felt like I wanted to sing and dance. I felt like an elephant had been lifted off my back.

"*Zengawii*," Frankie said. "It's magic, Zip."

He stuck his hand up in the air and we high-fived.

I started to skip. My luck had turned, and I had soy salami to thank for it.

CHAPTER 10

As you approach my mum's deli, your mouth starts to water whether you want it to or not. It doesn't matter if you've just eaten a thirty-four-course meal and are so full you feel like your stomach's going to explode, you get hungry all over again.

When you pull that glass door open and step inside, you are in the Kingdom of Smells. Sauerkraut and pickle smells come racing in from one side. Hot pastrami and corned beef pour in from the other. Rare roast beef, salami and sour green tomatoes circle in from behind. Your nose goes into overdrive. But wait a minute – what's that coming in from the counter? *Oh no!* Pickled herring in cream sauce with onions. Duck – it's nasty, nasty, nasty!

I have never understood who eats pickled herring. When everything else in The Crunchy Pickle is so incredibly delicious, why would anyone choose a grey, salty fish with white slime all over it? That stuff should have a shop of its own. Wait a minute, I know who eats it. Ms Adolf probably does. It matches her grey face.

Papa Pete says pickled herring in cream sauce is an acquired taste. I've noticed that grown-ups say that about everything that's truly disgusting, like lima beans, Brussels sprouts, beetroot, green peppers and movies in French.

The sandwich counter is at the back of the cafe, and in the front are the booths where the customers sit. Papa Pete picked out everything in The Crunchy Pickle himself. The booths are this special shade called periwinkle blue, which Papa Pete says he picked because it was the colour of my Grandma Jenny's eyes. He's so proud of how nice the deli looks. He always tells me that the booths are genuine leatherette – which is not as expensive as real leather, but not as cheap as plastic. There are always people inside The Crunchy Pickle, because it's such a cheerful place. And the normal food is extra-delicious. I'm not sure my mum's soy lunch meats are such a big draw.

When we came in, Carlos, the best sandwich maker in New York City, was behind the counter. Even though he's only twenty-three years old, he's worked at the deli for as long as I can remember. He started working there when he was still in high school, because his family had just come from Puerto Rico and they needed the money. Carlos and I always talk about baseball, and sometimes after work, we'll go over to the park and he gives me batting tips. Carlos has a great arm, and he throws a wicked curveball.

Carlos was building tongue and swiss cheese on rye bread for Mrs Wilcox. I've never understood why anyone would eat tongue. Think about it. A tongue has spent its whole life in a cow's mouth, covered in grass. I'm not even going to mention the cud-chewing part.

"Don't forget the extra Russian dressing on the side," Mrs Wilcox said to Carlos.

"I've already put two in the bag for you," Carlos answered. "And I put in extra pickles for Mr Wilcox. Really crunchy, just the way he likes them."

"*Muchas gracias*, Carlos," said Mrs Wilcox. I think she might have winked at him. All the women who come to The Crunchy Pickle love him. He's a pretty good-looking guy, with his shiny black hair and diamond stud earring. He always wears bright red socks, no matter what else he has on. Frankie says he must have a lot of confidence to wear bright red socks, even with shorts.

As he handed Mrs Wilcox her takeaway, Carlos flashed us a big grin. He's always happy to see us.

"Hey, Hankito," he said. "I saved you a black-and-white." He pulled an oversized biscuit that's half vanilla icing, half chocolate off the tray. It's my favourite because there are so many ways to eat it. You can take one bite and get both chocolate and vanilla. You can break it in half, eat all the chocolate and then vanilla. Or you can start on the chocolate, take a rest and then have some vanilla.

"Frankie, my man," Carlos said. "Here's your oatmeal-raisin." Frankie's mum wants him to eat wholegrains, so he's got really into oatmeal-and-raisin biscuits. They're the most healthy-sounding biscuits in the display case.

Carlos turned to Ashley. "*Ah, bonita,* I got your favourite, too," he said. Then he gave Ashley a sugar biscuit covered with rainbow-coloured sprinkles. "A beautiful biscuit for a beautiful young lady."

"And what do you want, little man?" Carlos asked Robert.

"Actually, I don't eat sugar," said Robert. "It causes tooth decay."

"Is that what happened to that tooth on the side there? Sugar got it?" Carlos asked Robert.

"No, that was an incisor that had to be removed because it was blocking the molar behind it. My dentist says I have an overcrowded mouth."

"You have an overcrowded brain," said Frankie.

We all laughed and spat bits of biscuit everywhere. A few of Ashley's sprinkles got stuck on the glass case.

"This is no laughing matter," Robert went on. "If your teeth are too close together, it traps food particles that create plaque, which hardens and causes decay, not to mention gum disease."

"Hey, little man, you shouldn't talk about that stuff. It's gross."

"That's OK, Carlos," Ashley said. "We're used to it. Robert says anything, anywhere, at any time."

We threw our rucksacks down on one of the empty tables and sat down to finish our biscuits. My father went to his usual corner booth where he keeps a stash of *New York Times* crossword-puzzle books. As Carlos brought him his favourite drink, a cup of hot water with lemon, my mother came out from the back of the shop. She was wearing her white headband, which means she's in her cooking mode. She has lots of blonde, curly hair, and when she cooks, food splatters in her hair and stays there. Once she had so much chocolate icing in her hair that she looked like she had brown hair. The headband keeps her hair clean and blonde.

"Hi, kids," she said. "How was school?"

"Fine," we all said at once – probably a little too quickly.

"How'd the spelling contest go?" she asked me.

"It was incredible, Mum. Remember the trouble I had with 'rhythm' last night? I nailed that word today."

"Good for you! Anything else interesting happen today?"

"Nope," I answered, barely looking at her. OK, I admit it, I felt a little guilty not telling her about my school report. But if you think about it, there was really no need for me to feel guilty about my answer. She asked if anything interesting had happened, and I said no. I don't happen to find getting a really bad report interesting, so technically, I wasn't lying.

"So, how's the soy salami coming along?" I asked, changing the subject as quickly as I could.

"Papa Pete and I are having an argument over it," she answered. "He doesn't think it has enough flavour. He went to get more garlic."

"I'm so interested to know all about your recipe, Mum," I said.

"Since when?" she asked, giving me a strange look.

"Since ... uh ... last Tuesday," I said. "Or maybe it was Wednesday. Yeah, it was Wednesday when I realized that I should know a lot more about what's in the lunch meats you make."

Just then, the cafe door swung open and in came Heather Payne and her mother. Heather Payne is the most perfect girl in our grade. Her mother was smiling. Actually, she was beaming. I knew that spelled trouble for me.

"We're here to get a special biscuit for my straight-*A* student," Mrs Payne said. "Heather got a perfect school report today."

My mother slowly turned her head in my direction. The silence hung in the air like boiled cabbage fumes.

"*Today* is school report day?" she asked, staring at me with eyes that practically burned a hole in my T-shirt. "I guess that little detail must have slipped your mind, Hank."

"Mum, you know that happens," I said. "My mind is slippery."

I gave her that big smile, the one that shows my top and bottom teeth. Frankie calls it The Attitude Grin. She wasn't buying it.

"I think we should continue this conversation in the back room," she said.

"No problem." I tried to sound casual.

"Bring your rucksack, Hank."

It occurred to me that I had better bring my friends, too. I picked up my rucksack and motioned for everyone to follow me.

"What are you going to do, Zip?" Frankie whispered.

"I have no idea," I said with a shrug.

The back room is where all the cooking equipment is: big, shiny ovens for baking, long

236

wooden counters for slicing and big bowls for making potato salad and coleslaw. It's the main kitchen, but it's also my mum's laboratory, where she makes up new recipes. I noticed that several of her big meat grinders were going, probably mixing up the recipes she and Papa Pete were working on.

No sooner were we in the back room than my mum spun around on her heels and said, "Let's have it."

"By *it*, I assume you mean my school report?" I asked, stalling for time.

"Hank, don't play with me."

"Right, OK," I said. "I'm sure it's here in my rucksack."

I dropped to my knees and started to empty my book bag as quickly as I could. I dumped everything out on the floor. While I was taking everything out, my mum walked over to check the machines that were grinding up her mystery meat. She mixed the ingredients up with a spatula and then came back.

Of course, I knew where my report was. I had tucked the big, brown manila envelope deep inside the secret zip pocket in which I keep my pencils. I was just pretending that I couldn't find it.

The room was quiet, except for the whirring of the meat grinder churning up the mystery meat and that sound of papers rattling as I emptied my book bag.

"Oh, there's my science workbook," I said, stalling for time. "We're learning such interesting things in science. We've almost finished our unit on astronomy. The solar system is so amazing, isn't it, Ashley?"

I motioned for Ashley to talk to my mum to keep her distracted.

"Why, yes, it is, Mrs Zipzer," Ashley said. "Did you know that they might have discovered another planet no one even knew was there?" I didn't hear the rest of what Ashley was saying, because I was putting my plan in motion.

I pulled the manila envelope with the report and Ms Adolf's letter inside out of the zip pocket and slipped it to Frankie.

Frankie gave me a look that asked, "What am I supposed to do with this?"

"Get rid of it," I whispered.

I turned to my mum, a look of surprise on my face.

"My report's not in here," I said, with shock in my voice. "Maybe I dropped it on the pavement while we were walking from school. And, you know, pigeons love to swoop down and pick up paper. They shred it with their beaks and use it to build their nests. I saw one do that on the Discovery Kids channel."

"Hank," my mother said, "I'm waiting."

I rummaged around in my rucksack some more. Out of the corner of my eye, I saw Frankie turn and hand my report to Ashley.

"Frankie," I said, "you don't happen to have my report, do you?"

Frankie held up both his hands to show that they were empty. "Why would I have your school report?"

Ashley took that opportunity to take the report and pass it on to Robert. Robert took it and looked for someone to pass it on to. But I was out of friends. There was no one left to pass it to. Then Robert did a brilliant thing. Maybe the most brilliant thing he's ever done in his bony little life. He edged over behind my mother and very quietly dropped the entire envelope into the whirring meat grinder.

I watched in amazement as my report disappeared into the beige mixture – all those *D*s becoming the new ingredients of soy salami.

My mother was losing patience.

"Henry!"

"Mum," I said, "I don't see it anywhere. Honestly, my school report has disappeared before my very eyes."

And I wasn't even lying.

CHAPTER 11

Papa Pete rushed in, carrying a brown grocery bag.

"Well, if it isn't my grandchildren," he said, giving us each a kiss on the top of the head. Papa Pete knows that I'm the only one who's actually related to him, but he calls all of us his grandkids anyway.

"Sorry I couldn't pick you up today, Hankie," he said to me. "I had to come to your mother's rescue."

"Pop, Hank and I were just having an important conversation," my mum said.

"What is so important that it can't wait until tomorrow?" he asked. "Now is not the time to talk,

Randi. Now is the time to grind meat. If we don't get some zing into that paste you're calling a salami, your order from Mr Gristediano is going to go out the window."

Papa Pete slipped his butcher's apron over his head and began to sharpen his chopping knife.

"Papa Pete, I need to talk to you sometime," I whispered. "It's about my grades."

"We'll talk tomorrow," he whispered back. "No time to talk now," he said in a loud voice, so no one could see we were whispering. "I've got to save your mother from ruining her business."

"Pop, I'm not ruining the business," my mum said to him.

Papa Pete turned off the meat grinder that was chewing up the last of my school report. He took off the bowl, gave it a sniff and turned up his nose. I tried to get a look inside the bowl. I could see a few chunks of brown manila paper blended in with the beige soy mixture.

"You will if you try to pass off that soy glue in there as salami," Papa Pete said, shoving the bowl to the end of the counter. "It looks terrible and it tastes like nothing."

"It tastes like soy," my mother said.

"Which tastes like nothing," Papa Pete insisted. "I rest my case."

He reached inside the brown grocery bag and pulled out several long strands of fresh, purple garlic.

"Now, this is the food of the gods," he said. "Garlic. This will make your taste buds stand up and salute."

My mother shook her head. "Pop, that much garlic will overwhelm the taste of the soy," she said.

"Nonsense, Randi," he answered. "Garlic puts hair on your chest. Isn't that right, men?" He looked at Frankie and me and winked.

We laughed. That's what must have happened to Papa Pete, because he has more hair on his chest than a gorilla – on his face, too. He has a moustache that's so big he calls it his handlebars.

"Let's get to work, Randi," he said. "I'll help you whip up a batch of salami that tastes like something."

"All right, Pop." My mum sighed. I could tell she had given up the fight. When Papa Pete has a plan, it's pretty hard to talk him out of it. "Hank, we'll continue this conversation tomorrow," she said.

That was good enough for me. I had bought myself another day to figure things out.

Papa Pete reached into his pocket and pulled out a twenty-dollar note. He rolled it up and slipped it into the palm of my hand.

"On the way home, stop in at McKelty's and get yourself and my other grandkids some root-beer floats," he said. "And tell The Chopped Livers I'll bowl tonight, but I'll be a little late. Your mother and I have some high-level delicatessen work to do."

"So you and Mum aren't going to use the stuff in there for Mr Gristediano's salami?" I asked, pointing to the bowl with my report in it.

"I wouldn't give that to a dog," said Papa Pete. "The only thing that stuff is good for is to lie at the bottom of the rubbish bin."

As we left the back room, I gave Frankie and Ashley a big thumbs-up. My report was going bye-bye into the bin. This had worked out better than I could have hoped for.

"Robert, you're a genius," I whispered, slapping him on the back so hard that he almost fell over. He acts like such an adult I sometimes forget that Robert's just a pencil-neck eight-year-old. I could feel the bones in his back. He really should eat some more mashed potato or something.

"I have an IQ of one hundred and thirty-seven," Robert said. "Technically, a genius is someone with an IQ of one-hundred and forty and above."

"Do you ever lighten up, Robert?" asked Frankie.

"Actually, no," said Robert.

My dad walked us home, and we had the greatest afternoon. We stopped and had root-beer floats at McKelty's Roll 'N Bowl. When we got back to our apartment, Emily wasn't there. She was playing at her friend Jenna's house, so we had the place to ourselves. Frankie and I played video games while Ashley made a rhinestone mouse mat for her mum's birthday. Robert helped my dad with his crossword puzzle. When Robert told him that a "spider relative with two pairs of eyes" was a horseshoe crab, I thought my dad was going to blast right out of his chair. Those thirteen letters put him in such a good mood that he let us watch cartoons on TV until it was time for everyone to go home for dinner.

My mum was really happy when she got back from work. She was so filled with her salami dreams that she seemed to have forgotten all about my report. She could hardly wait until the next day. She said she had a feeling Mr Gristediano was going to give her a big order. If he did, she promised to take us all on a holiday somewhere. She suggested a weekend in Vermont. My dad wanted to go fly-fishing in Canada. I voted for Costa Rica, because I've always wanted to see a real rainforest. Besides, I figured that if they found out about my report and got really mad, I could hide in the rain forest and live on bananas. Maybe a monkey family would adopt me. Emily said she wasn't going anywhere there weren't crocodiles. I suggested we leave Emily at home.

We ate tuna-melts and chicken noodle soup for dinner.

"So, when will we find out Mr Gristediano's decision?" I asked.

"Carlos is delivering the trays of salami to

him tomorrow morning," my mum said. "Mr Gristediano is having all his managers over for a tasting party. If they like it, we should hear straight away."

"They have to like it," I said. "I'm sure you and Papa Pete came up with a great recipe."

"Actually," my mum said, "I have a little secret. Don't tell Papa Pete this, but I went back to my first version of soy salami. I thought his had way too much garlic."

I stopped eating.

"You don't mean that original batch of salami," I said. "The one you were making when I was there at about, say, three-thirty-five?"

"Yes," my mum said. "That's the one. That's the winner. I asked Carlos to roll it up and put it in the fridge. He'll slice it tomorrow morning and deliver the platter first thing."

Oh no. That was the batch of salami with the special ingredient – my school report. I reached for a glass of water and gulped it down all at once.

"Is anything wrong, honey?" my mum asked.

"Wrong?" I asked. "What could possibly be wrong?"

CHAPTER 12

"**May I be excused?**" I asked, trying to sound calm, which I wasn't.

"Don't you want dessert?" my mum asked. "I made carrot pudding."

"Wow, Mum," I said. "You really know how to use those vegetables. It's hard to say no to carrot pudding, but I've got to run, if you know what I mean." I glanced towards the bathroom. Parents never say no to the bathroom.

"Of course, darling," my mum said.

I shot out of my chair like a rocket and ran down the hall. My socks had no traction on the wooden floors, and I went flying like a speed skater right through the bathroom door. I landed on my backside, wedged between the toilet and the bath. I pulled myself up and turned on the cold water in the sink. I had to splash my face with cold water to stop my cheeks from twitching, which they do when I panic.

I needed to think clearly. Too many thoughts were running through my head all at once. *Why hadn't I just told my parents that I'd got a lousy report in the first place? Why did Robert have to throw my report in the meat grinder? What was he thinking? What's wrong with just a regular bin? Would it be against the law for Robert to do a normal thing for once in his life?*

I splashed more water on my face. My cheeks had pretty much stopped twitching, except for the right one, which still moved every now and then.

Lying is hard, I thought. You have to keep everything straight, and that's hard for me normally. Then I had a radical idea. Maybe I should just tell my parents the whole truth – that I'm not cut out for school. That no matter how hard I try, I'm just never going to make it as a student. My mum would be sad and my dad would be mad, but I'd tell them,

"Hey, you've got Emily. She's brilliant. I'm wired differently, and my wires are crossed."

Just thinking about that made my cheeks start twitching all over again. The cold water wasn't helping. I needed a clear head to sort this all out. I slipped out of the bathroom, went to the telephone and dialled Frankie's number. His dad answered.

"Hello, Dr Townsend," I said. "This is Hank. May I talk to Frankie?"

"He's just finishing dinner," Dr Townsend said. "Can he call you back?"

"Normally he could," I said, "but I have an emergency here. Not the kind with an ambulance or anything. It's the kind that could wait, but shouldn't."

"That sounds important, Hank," said Dr Townsend. "Hold on."

When Frankie got on the phone, I blurted it out: "Emergency meeting. Basement. Now. Pass it on."

I slammed down the phone, ran to my room and pulled on my shoes. There was something else I needed, but I couldn't remember what it was. It had just been *on* my mind and now it was *under* it. I looked around, hoping it would come to me.

I don't have time for forgetting now. Then, thank goodness, I saw my sweatshirt hanging on the back of my chair. That was it – my sweatshirt. I knew I wanted to take it, because the basement where our clubhouse is can get cold in November.

"I'm going downstairs to Frankie's," I called to my parents.

"I'll come with you," my mum said.

"You will? No! I mean, why?"

"It's yoga class night," my mum said. Frankie's mum holds her yoga classes in their living room.

"Oh, right."

"We're going to learn a new position. It's called the cobra."

"Sounds dangerous," I said. "Don't bite yourself."

My mum laughed. I thought about what a nice, cheerful person she is and for a minute considered telling her about my marks right then and there. Maybe she'd be really sweet and understanding. Then my dad walked into the room.

"I'm going play Scrabble with Emily," my dad said. "Hank, why don't you join us?"

Right, me play Scrabble – the guy who got a *D*

in spelling would play Scrabble with a girl genius and a crossword-puzzle nut. Sometimes I think my father doesn't have any idea who I am. Any thought I had of telling my parents about my marks went right out the window.

I escaped into the hall and pushed the lift button. It always takes a while to get up to the tenth floor. When it landed, I pulled the door open and was face to face with our neighbour, Mrs Fink.

"Why, thank you, Hank." She smiled as she got out and I noticed with relief that she was wearing her false teeth, which she doesn't always do. "You're growing into such a gentleman."

My mother came into the hall just as Mrs Fink stepped out of the lift.

"Hello, Randi," Mrs Fink said. *Uh-oh.* This was bad timing, because Mrs Fink's "Hello, Randi" usually turns into a forty-five-minute conversation about what eating spicy food does to her digestion. I had a crisis on my hands, and there was no time now for intestine talk.

"Mum, you don't want to be late for class," I said, pulling her into the lift. "The cobra is waiting."

As we were travelling down to the fourth floor, my mum looked at me funny.

"You seem nervous tonight," she said. "Is anything going on?"

"Nope," I said, not looking her in the eye.

She pointed to a spot on her hand and smiled. "I know you like the back of my hand, mister," she said. "Something's cooking."

Thank goodness the lift jerked to a stop on Frankie's floor and I didn't have to answer her. Frankie yanked the door open and was about to say something to me, when he saw my mum. Instead, he just gestured politely to his front door.

"Go right in, Mrs Z.," he said. "There's great karma in there." You can always count on Frankie to be cool in a hot situation.

After my mum was out, he jumped into the lift with me. I pushed the *B* button about ten times, as if that would get us to the basement faster.

"Is Ashley coming?" I asked.

"On her way," he said.

Finally, we reached the basement. As we walked out of the lift, I could tell that someone had just finished doing laundry. It was warm and the air smelled like soapsuds and bleach. We passed the laundry room and went into the storage room that we use as our clubhouse. Ashley was waiting with a chocolate-chip cookie for me and an oatmeal-pecan one for Frankie.

"What's the big emergency?" she asked.

I dropped myself into one of the sofas that line the wall of our clubhouse.

"You're not going to believe this. You know the batch of soy salami that Robert dropped my school report into?"

"Tell me not to think what I'm thinking," said Frankie, "because what I'm thinking is a bad, bad think."

"I can't, Frankie, because I think I'm thinking what you're thinking."

"Will you guys stop thinking and talk to me?" screamed Ashley.

"My mum decided to send her original batch of salami to Mr Gristediano tomorrow," I said.

"I think I'm starting to think what you're

thinking," Ashley said. She twirled her long ponytail around in her fingers, the way she does when she's worried. When she wears pigtails, she twirls both of them, one with each hand.

I took a deep breath and spilled out the whole ugly truth.

"It's bad, guys," I said. "The salami that is being delivered at ten-thirty tomorrow morning is the very same one that has my report mushed and squished in it."

"Maybe it's not so bad," Ashley said, trying to sound upbeat. "Maybe the paper was ground up into tiny little bitsy bits and you can't even tell it's in there."

"Ashweena," said Frankie, "there's no way all that paper could get lost in the salami. We're talking a manila envelope, a report and a letter written on legal-size paper. I assume it was legal size. It's got to be. When you have so many nasty things to say, you use legal size."

I put my head in my hands.

"I'm sure the whole batch is ruined," I said. "Now my mum will lose the sale. Her hopes and dreams for the future of lunch meats will go right down the drain and it will be all my fault."

This was a total nightmare. I was single-handedly putting The Crunchy Pickle out of business. And I was still in trouble. Ms Adolf was going to want to see a signed report from my parents. Where was that supposed to come from? I'd have to Scotch tape twenty slices of salami together, and even then, you'd have to be really good at reading meat to decipher it.

"I am such a loser," I said, to no one in particular.

Frankie flopped down next to me.

"Snap out of it, Zip," he said. "You're not going to just sit there and let this happen. That's not the Hank Zipzer I know. Breathe, Zip. Let the oxygen flow to promote thinking."

"There's no way out of this," I said. "It's not like we can just find our way over to Mr Gristediano's flat – wherever that is – and happen to arrive just as Carlos is delivering the tray and bump into him so the salami goes all over the street and gets eaten by a dog and has to be replaced by a new batch."

"Actually, why not?" came a familiar, uninvited voice from the door.

We whipped around and there he was – Robert.

"When Napoleon invaded Russia, he took the shortest route – through France," said Robert.

"Who is Napoleon?" I snapped.

"He's dead," said Robert. "But when he wasn't, he was a very short French general."

"Great, Robert. What does a short, dead French general have to do with a platter of soy salami that is polluted with my rotten report?"

"I was just using him as an example of basic military strategy," Robert said. "Napoleon knew that the simplest plans are always the best."

"The boy may have a point," said Frankie, getting up off the sofa and starting to pace. "We cut off the delivery. We seize the polluted salami. We destroy it. We replace it with a good batch."

Frankie was excited now.

"Do you really think this could work?" I asked.

"We're going to make it work," Frankie said. "And we'll make it work with style. Don't forget, Zip, we are the Magik 3."

"So?"

"So that means we add our own magic touch to this plan, to make sure your mum gets the biggest order possible."

"You mean we get to do our magic show?" Ashley asked.

"I think we should pretend we are the entertainment, sent by The Crunchy Pickle to perform feats of magic for the guests as they munch," Frankie said.

"Cool," said Ashley. "I'll do my cherry stem trick."

"Let's hold that for another performance, Ashweena," answered Frankie. "The way I see this performance, we'll cover the salami tray with my cape. True, my cape may smell like salami for a couple of months after, but I'm willing to make the sacrifice. Once we're in Mr Gristediano's flat, we'll gather everyone around and *Zengawii*! I'll pull off my cape and the salami will appear."

"Then we just sit back and wait for the big order to come in," Ashley said.

"I love it," I said.

Ashley gave Frankie a high five. Even Robert nodded with approval.

"You tell your pal Napoleon that he's got nothing on me," Frankie said to Robert.

"Actually, I would tell him but, as I already

pointed out, he's dead," Robert reminded us.

"It's a brilliant plan," said Ashley. "Don't you think so, Hank?"

I didn't know if it was a brilliant plan or not. But I did know one thing. It was our best shot. It was our *only* shot.

CHAPTER 13

We couldn't leave anything to chance. There was no room for mistakes.

It took us more than an hour to work out all the details. Ashley got some paper and wrote down the whole schedule. This is what it looked like:

FRIDAY NIGHT

<u>9.00 p.m.</u>: call Papa Pete and ask him to meet us in front of our building at 9.45 a.m. Saturday.

<u>9.15 p.m.</u>: ask parents if we can take Cheerio for a walk in the park with Papa Pete the next morning.

9.30 p.m.: phone one another to make any final arrangements.

SATURDAY MORNING

9.45 a.m.: meet Papa Pete in front of building. Don't forget Cheerio!

9.46 a.m.: walk to The Crunchy Pickle. Arrive before ten o'clock and hide outside.

10.00 a.m.: Carlos leaves The Crunchy Pickle for his delivery. Follow him to Mr Gristediano's flat.

10.20 a.m.: Carlos arrives at Mr Gristediano's flat. Turn Cheerio loose on him.

10.21 a.m.: Cheerio runs into Carlos and starts to chew on his trouser leg. Knocks tray out of his hands. Salami spills on ground.

10.22 a.m.: Cheerio eats salami, with help from neighbouring dogs.

10.25 a.m.: Carlos goes back to The Crunchy Pickle for a new tray of soy salami, the one that Papa Pete made.

10.27 a.m.: Frankie puts on cape and we turn into Magik 3.

10.30 a.m.: go up to Mr Gristediano's apartment and apologize for the late delivery.

10.35 a.m.: entertain store managers with magic show while Carlos is getting the new tray.

11.00 a.m.: Carlos arrives with tray of all new salami.

11.05 a.m.: smile at all the guests and make sure they love the salami. Tell them how much their order means to The Crunchy Pickle.

11.10 a.m.: leave Mr Gristediano's apartment.

11.25 a.m.: arrive back at our flat. Notice strange smell coming from Cheerio (probably wind from salami).

11.26 a.m.: open windows.

11.30 a.m.: wait for the phone call placing the order.

11.35 a.m.: celebrate!

I'm telling you, this was a plan that even Napoleon would have been proud of. Now all we had to do was pull it off.

CHAPTER 14

Papa Pete agreed to meet us in the morning. He was curious to know what all the mystery was about, but I told him I'd fill him in later. He laughed and said he needed a little excitement in his life.

I woke up early, which is something I don't usually do on Saturday mornings. At breakfast, my mum and dad were so nervous, wondering whether or not Mr Gristediano would like the salami, that they didn't pay much attention to where I said I was going. As long as I was with Papa Pete, they knew I'd be safe. Frankie, Ashley and Robert had got the go-ahead from their parents, too.

I had memorized our timetable. At exactly

9.40 a.m., I found Cheerio's lead and went to the closet to get my coat. It wasn't in the closet.

"Has anyone seen my green coat?" I yelled.

"How many times have I told you, Hank? You have to keep track of your own things," my father answered from the living room.

Now is not a good time for a lecture, I thought. I started to run around like a crazy person, looking for my coat. I found it on a chair in the hall, just outside Emily's room. There was only one slight problem – Katherine was sitting on it, sound asleep.

"Emily!" I yelled. "Your lizard is on my coat."

"Just lift her up," called Emily from her room. "She won't bite."

"I'm not touching that thing," I said. "I'll get warts."

Emily marched out of her room. "People say that about frogs, not iguanas," she said. "And besides, it's a myth. You don't catch warts from frogs. Warts are caused by a virus."

"Fine," I said. "You and Robert can discuss that in detail sometime. I'm sure he'd find it fascinating. Now could you please just pick up that reptile and get her off my coat?"

"I can't," said Emily. "I've just painted my nails and they're still wet." Emily has this habit of painting each of her nails a different colour. She thinks it's part of her "look". If that's her look, I think she should look elsewhere.

"Emily," I said. "I'm going to count to three and then tell Mum. One … two…"

"OK, you don't have to be so bossy about it," Emily said, lifting Katherine up and putting her on her shoulder.

I put my coat on quickly. I was worried that I was going to be late. Then I grabbed Cheerio and opened the door to leave. I turned to say goodbye to my dad. Suddenly, Katherine, who must have fallen in love with my coat, jumped off Emily and ran across the living room after me. She grabbed on to my trousers and crawled up my leg and on to the coat, digging her claws into the fabric as if it was her long-lost mother or something. I got scared and yelled so loudly that Mrs Fink came running out of her flat into the hall. She was in her big pink dressing gown, and she didn't have her teeth in.

I spun around like a madman, trying to unhitch Katherine from my back. It must have worked, because the next thing I knew, Katherine had jumped to the floor. She looked around for a place to go and saw somewhere she liked. Unfortunately, that place was Mrs Fink. Katherine leapt on to the bottom of her big pink bathrobe and crawled all the way up Mrs Fink until she stopped about three inches from her face.

"*Heeeeeeeeeeeeeelp!*" Mrs Fink shrieked in a voice that sounded like a wild hyena I once heard on a National Geographic special.

"*Someone heeeeeeeeeeeeeelp me!*"

My mum was the first one out in the hall.

"Emily!" she screamed when she saw Katherine hanging off Mrs Fink's chest. "Come out here right now."

"I'm painting my nails," Emily called back.

"Now!" shouted my father, who had joined the group in the hall.

The doors of the other two flats on our floor flew open. Little Tyler King stuck his head out from behind his mother. He was wearing his Spider-Man pyjamas.

"Mummy! Mummy!" he screamed, when he saw what was going on. "There's a big rat on Mrs Fink's boobies."

Mr Park from Flat 10D came out and tried to help. He reached out for Katherine, but when she saw him coming, Katherine whipped out her tongue and waved it in front of him. He jumped back, like any sane person would if they saw that long, ugly tongue.

"Call the police!" cried Mrs Fink.

"Call the fire brigade!" called Mr Park.

"Please be calm, everyone!" said my mother. "Katherine won't hurt you."

By now, Emily had arrived on the scene. "Ohhh, she likes you," Emily said to Mrs Fink.

"Well, I don't like her!" screamed Mrs Fink.

"She doesn't go to anyone she doesn't like," Emily said.

Emily came over to Mrs Fink and slowly reached out for Katherine. But Katherine liked it there on Mrs Fink's chest, and she refused to go to Emily. She dug her claws into the dressing gown and hung on. It was a pathetic sight. Poor Mrs Fink was pressed up against the wall, her arms spread out like giant eagle wings. She was too scared to move. The only things she moved were her eyeballs, and they were popping out of her head like something you'd see in a cartoon. She looked down at Katherine and whimpered.

"Nice lizard. Go away now."

Katherine stared at Mrs Fink with her beady eyes, then suddenly stuck her tongue out. Then Mrs Fink, for some unknown reason, stuck her tongue out at Katherine. Katherine did it back to her. Mrs Fink stuck her tongue out again, this time a little further. Katherine waited a second, then shot her tongue right back at Mrs Fink.

"Look," Emily whispered to me. "They're communicating. It's like a dance."

"The tongue tango," I moaned. "That's so gross, Emily."

"I think it's sweet," Emily said, "and if you didn't have a brain the size of a pea, you'd think so too."

"I have to go," I said to Emily. "I'm meeting Papa Pete downstairs and I can't be late."

"You can't go now," Emily answered, grabbing on to my sleeve to stop me. "Look! They're having a breakthrough."

I couldn't believe what I saw. Katherine stuck out her tongue and actually licked Mrs Fink on the cheek. Mrs Fink touched Katherine's head with her index finger and smiled, showing her pink gums. I guess that's something that appeals to iguanas, because Katherine's tongue shot out and licked Mrs Fink again.

"Look, Mummy! They're kissing," said Tyler King. "*Eeewww*, that's so yucky!"

"I think it's the sweetest thing I've ever seen," said Emily. She sounded like she was going to cry.

This was too much for me.

"Bill, please," I said.

"Where are you going?" Emily asked.

"Listen, I'd love to stay and get all mushy with you reptiles, but Cheerio and I have important business with Papa Pete." I looked at my watch. "Got to run!"

I really was late. Katherine's little hallway adventure had cost us ten minutes. I grabbed Cheerio and ran as fast as I could down the stairs.

CHAPTER 15

I've known Mrs Fink all my life, and I think she's a nice lady. But watching her and Katherine doing the tongue tango was just more than any guy should ever have to see.

Ashley, Frankie and Robert had already met up with Papa Pete outside. The four of them were waiting for me under the awning of our building.

"You're late, Zip," Frankie said. "What happened to you?"

"Our iguana fell in love with Mrs Fink," I answered, knowing that would shut him up, and it did. He just grabbed his stomach and pretended he was going to throw up.

"Let's go," said Ashley. "We're late."

"Excuse me, lady and gentlemen. May I ask what it is we're late for?" asked Papa Pete.

"We have to go to the deli," I told Papa Pete. "I don't have time to explain now, because we have to get there before Carlos leaves on his delivery run."

"He leaves at ten," said Papa Pete. "That gives us exactly five minutes."

We took off down 78th Street towards Broadway. Cheerio tried to keep up with us. His four short legs moved as fast as they could, but they didn't cover much ground. He looked like he was on one of those treadmills people use at the gym. When we came to our first red light, I picked up Cheerio and tucked him under my arm. We waited. It was the longest red light in the history of electricity.

"Don't look at it," Ashley said. "I swear it makes it stay red longer."

We all turned away. When we looked back, it was still red.

I turned to Frankie in desperation.

"Say your magic words," I begged.

Frankie faced the light, put his hands in the air and said, "*Zengawii*." The light changed from red to green.

"I am all-powerful," said Frankie, half believing it.

"Actually," said Robert, "the light is set for a minute and twenty-two seconds depending on traffic flow."

"Shut up, Robert," we all said, as we always do.

We crossed Broadway and ran the last block to The Crunchy Pickle. It was one of those crisp, cool New York mornings, a perfect morning for running. In summer in New York, you don't feel like running because it's hot and you get all sweaty before you even start. In winter, it's so cold that when you run and breathe hard, the air stings the inside of your nose. But when you run on an autumn morning, well, it feels just right.

We got to the deli, and I pushed the glass door open. Carlos wasn't there, but Vladimir was working behind the counter, putting toothpicks into cheese squares. Vladimir Olefski is our weekend cook and sandwich man. He's from

Russia, and he speaks English with a thick accent. I was scared of Vlady at first, because he never smiles and also because he has a lot of reddish-blondish hair growing out of his ears. It's not actually that much hair, but as far as I'm concerned, *any* hair growing out of your ears is a lot. I remember thinking that Vlady reminded me of a werewolf I saw once on a late-night movie when I slept over at Frankie's. Papa Pete tells me not to look at his ears. He says that when a man can stuff a cabbage like Vlady can stuff a cabbage, what's a little ear hair?

Vlady had his back to us, and he was singing this Russian song he always sings. It is the saddest song you've ever heard. Once I asked Vlady what it was about.

"A man looks for fish in Volga River," he said. "No fish there, so he must eat only snow and stale bread. My family sings this song at parties, and we cry like babies." Those Olefskis must be some really fun party animals.

"Hi, Vlady," I said. "Where's Carlos?"

"He is left," Vlady said.

Oh no! "How long ago?"

"Many minutes before," Vlady answered in his thick Russian accent.

We had counted on following Carlos. How else could we get to Mr Gristediano's? We didn't even have his address.

"This is bad," said Ashley. "A real fly in the ointment."

"No flies here," Vlady snapped. "I keep place clean."

"Vlady," said Frankie, saying every syllable very clearly. "Do you know the address where Carlos went?"

"He write on paper," Vlady said, pointing to a pad of paper we keep by the phone to write down deliveries.

Ashley grabbed the pad. The top sheet was blank. Obviously, Carlos had taken Mr Gristediano's address with him.

"Another fly in the ointment," Ashley muttered.

"Pardon, missy," Vlady said, his blue eyes squinting at Ashley from under his big red eyebrows. "I say *NO FLIES*."

Frankie looked at the blank pad.

"Carlos must go through a lot of pencils," he said. "He writes hard. Look, every word leaves an impression on the paper underneath."

That was all I needed to hear.

"Vlady," I said, "can I borrow your pencil?"

He took the pencil from behind his ear and handed it to me. I wiped it off quickly, to make sure it didn't have any loose ear hair on it. Then I laid it on its side and began rubbing the lead back and forth over the blank piece of paper. The paper turned grey, except the parts on which Carlos's pencil had written the address, which stayed white. As I shaded over the whole page, little by little the address popped out.

"I've got it," I yelled, looking at the piece of paper. "Five-forty-one Riverside Drive, Flat 4B."

I ripped the page off the pad.

"Let's jet," I said. I looked around for Papa Pete. He had slid into one of the booths with a cup of coffee. "Come on, Papa Pete. We've got to hurry."

"I just got myself a Danish," he said.

"Can you take it to go?" Frankie asked.

"Is it absolutely necessary?" asked Papa Pete.

"Abso-one-hundred-per-cent-lutely," said Frankie.

"In that case, I think I can," said Papa Pete. He wrapped the Danish in a napkin and shoved it into his pocket.

"Papa Pete, you are the greatest," I said, dashing to the door and holding it open for him.

"Is someone going to tell me what all this is about?" he asked.

"No time now," I said. "Later."

"OK, Hankie," said Papa Pete. "The mystery continues."

"Close door," Vlady called after us. "No flies."

I tucked Cheerio under my arm and we tore out on to the street and headed down towards Riverside Drive. It was about four blocks to Mr Gristediano's flat.

"We'll never get there before Carlos does," Frankie said.

"I think we have a chance," I said. I happen to know that Carlos is not the fastest delivery guy in town. He is the nicest and the best dressed, but not the fastest.

"I hope I don't get an asthma attack," said Robert, panting hard.

Ashley turned to him and said, "You don't have time, Robert."

"Oh, right," he said.

It may sound amazing to you, but Papa Pete had no trouble keeping up with us. He's in great shape. He's big, but he's solid muscle.

"It's from the bowling," he always says. "Keeps a man fit." I'm sure that walking up and down the stairs to McKelty's Roll 'N Bowl doesn't hurt, either.

We reached 541 Riverside Drive. It was a fancy building with two carved lions at the front. The doorman was leaning on one of them, picking his teeth with a toothpick. He didn't look friendly.

I walked up to him, but before I could open my mouth, old Robert butted in. "Excuse me, Mr Riverside," he said.

Frankie whipped around and stared at Robert.

"What do you think you're doing?" he whispered.

"I'm calling the man by his name," said Robert. "It's good manners."

"That's not his name, numbskull," said Frankie. "That's the name of the building embroidered on his coat."

"How was I supposed to know?" asked Robert. "I'm only in third grade."

Right. Now he was in the third grade. When he wants to bore you with the name of every mountain range in Asia, he's a college professor, but when he screws up, he's just a third-grader.

I turned to the doorman.

"Has the delivery from The Crunchy Pickle arrived yet for apartment 4B?" I asked.

"No."

Just as I had thought. Carlos was late. *Do I know my delivery guys or what?*

"That's excellent," I said, "because we have a very important matter to discuss with the delivery person who's bringing Mr Gristediano's platters."

"Good for you," the doorman said, adjusting the toothpick in his mouth. "Who's Mr Gristediano?"

"He lives in Flat 4B," I said.

"Says you," he answered.

"No, really," I said. "Take a look."

I reached into my pocket and pulled out the paper from the pad at the deli.

"See," I said, pointing to the address. "It's right there in black and white. Five-forty-one Riverside Drive."

He glanced down at the paper, then back at me.

"Funny," he said. "Looks to me like that says *four*-fifty-one Riverside Drive."

I looked down at the paper and stared at it for a minute. I couldn't believe my eyes. It *did* say 451. I must have flipped the numbers around. How could I have been so stupid? I can't even read three numbers the right way round.

The truth is, I flip numbers around a lot. Sometimes I flip letters around too. Most of the time, I don't even know I'm doing it.

I hit my hand on the side of my head, as if I could knock some sense into my stupid brain.

"What is wrong with me?" I asked.

Papa Pete put his hand on mine. He has big hands, and when he touches you, it makes you feel safe.

"What's with the hitting yourself in the head?" he asked.

"I'm the stupidest person in the world," was all I could answer.

"This isn't a tragedy, champ," he said. "You just mixed up a couple of numbers. Worse things could happen."

"You don't understand, Papa Pete," I said. "Now we'll never catch up with Carlos. In fact, he's probably already delivered the salami platter to Mr Gristediano."

"So?" asked Papa Pete. "What's wrong with that?"

"Everything. Once Mr Gristediano tastes that salami, it's over for us."

"What are you talking about?" he asked. "The salami is delicious. I made it myself."

"No," I tried to explain. "You made another batch, not that one. There's something terribly wrong with the salami Carlos is taking to Mr Gristediano. I ruined it. And now I've ruined Mum's business and her whole future too. It's all my fault."

I could feel the tears welling up at the corners

of my eyes. Papa Pete looked from Frankie to Ashley to Robert, then back to me.

"Does everyone here know what's going on but me?" he asked.

They nodded.

"Then I think we have to talk," said Papa Pete. "It's time for this mystery to end."

CHAPTER 16

We sat down on a bench in Riverside Park. A couple of little kids were playing near by. They held hands and spun around in a circle until they got so dizzy that they fell down on the grass. Then they laughed like maniacs, got up, spun around and fell down again. I love to hear little kids laugh. They sound like they don't have a problem in the world. I watched them for a minute, wishing I were that little again.

"Now, suppose you tell me exactly what is going on," Papa Pete began.

"I don't know where to start," I said.

"Try the beginning," said Papa Pete.

I took a deep breath. Once I'd started talking, it felt so good to have the truth all come tumbling out. I told Papa Pete about my school report and the three Ds. I explained that I was too ashamed to show that report to my parents, so I had pretended to lose it. When I got to the part about the deli and said that we hadn't planned to throw my report in the meat grinder, Papa Pete held up his hand.

"Are you about to tell me that your school report card is ground up in the salami that went to Mr Gristediano?"

I nodded.

"Actually, there's a letter from Ms Adolf and a large manila envelope in there too," Robert added.

"So that's the big rush to get to Mr Gristediano's – to get the salami back."

Papa Pete had certainly figured it out fast. I wondered if he had ever done anything this bad when he was younger.

"We all feel terrible," Ashley said, "because we were part of this too."

Papa Pete gathered us around him.

"I want you to listen to me, grandkids," he said.

"People are just people. They make mistakes. A guy orders a tuna on rye, and you bring him a roast beef on wheat. It happens."

Papa Pete turned to me.

"But this I know, grandson of mine. You can't lie to cover up your mistakes. You start with one little lie and it gets bigger and bigger, and before you know it, it's taken over everything. It's like dropping one little piece of herring in a tub of macaroni cheese. Before long, the whole tub smells like fish. You follow what I'm saying?"

Actually, he'd kind of lost me on the herring in the macaroni story, but I think I got the general idea. He was saying that once you tell a lie, you just create more and more trouble for yourself. And boy, was he ever right.

"So we're going to fix this right now," he said. "Hank, you're going to go to Mr Gristediano's and get the salami back. We don't want anyone to be ill. Then you're going to tell your parents the truth."

In my heart, I knew Papa Pete was right. As much as I didn't want to confess, it had to be done.

Frankie put his hand on my shoulder.

"Zip, mate, I wish there was a magic word I could say to make this better," he said.

"There is a magic word," said Papa Pete, "and it works every time. It's called the *truth*."

CHAPTER 17

It was two blocks to Mr Gristediano's apartment, and they seemed like the two longest blocks in the entire city. Now it was Papa Pete who was hurrying, because he was worried that someone would eat one of my *D*s, which might then cause the Big *D*, that *D* being diarrhoea. I guess eating paper will do that to you, unless you happen to be a goat.

We tried running up Riverside Drive, but Cheerio was slowing us down again. He was stopping and sniffing every fire hydrant, tree and doorway along the street. At home, he's happy just to lie on his back and stare at the ceiling, but now, when we were in a hurry, he'd suddenly turned into Mr Curious.

"Come on, Cheerio, step on it," I said.

"Actually, he's checking to see where other dogs have marked their territory," Robert said.

"Robert, let's just say it like it is," said Frankie. "He's sniffing pee."

I picked up Cheerio and tucked him under my arm. He squirmed and wanted to jump out of my grasp, but I gave him no choice in the matter. Papa Pete was in front, running fast. He's pretty light on his feet for a guy who's going to be sixty-eight on 26 June.

Here's something I never realized before. Cheerio is heavy when you're running. By the time we reached 451 Riverside Drive, my right arm had fallen asleep. So had Cheerio. I wondered how he could sleep with all that shaking and bouncing going on.

We stopped to catch our breath, which you could actually see coming out of our mouths in little puffs of steam. The building doorman was standing inside, watching us through the fancy glass panes in the door.

"Papa Pete," I said. "Will you tell the doorman he's got to let us in right away?"

"You can do it," he said. "I'll wait downstairs. There's a nice sofa in the lobby."

"You're not coming?"

Papa Pete shook his head. "You know what you have to do," he said. "This is your mission. Accomplish it."

Papa Pete was right. I had got us into this mess and I had to get us out of it. I marched up to the door, pushed it open and tried to look very important.

"Sir," I said to the doorman. "We're from The

Crunchy Pickle. We have to see Mr Gristediano on a matter of utmost importance."

"Says who?" the doorman answered, looking me up and down suspiciously. He obviously wasn't too impressed.

"Says all of us," said Frankie, stepping up to my defence. "You know those platters of salami that were delivered a little while ago? We need to take them back immediately. They're very dangerous."

"I've never heard of a dangerous salami before," the doorman said. "Except the one my brother-in-law Marvin ate once. Gave him so much wind he nearly blew himself up."

He laughed really loudly.

"Actually, sir, those salamis are filled with pulp," said Robert.

"Yeah," he said, "so was my brother-in-law Marvin." He laughed so hard that the gold buttons on his coat shook. "Hey, I'm just kidding with ya."

"So can we go up now?" Ashley asked, bringing the conversation back around. Ashley's good at getting down to business.

"I'll call and let them know you're coming."

I looked over at Papa Pete on the sofa. He gave me a quick thumbs-up. The doorman rang the button marked 4B.

"Yeah, I got some kids down here from The Crunchy Pickle," he said into the telephone. "They say they got to check on the cold cuts."

He paused and nodded, then turned to us.

"They're expecting you," he said. "Fourth floor. Lift's on your left."

Before he let us pass, he pointed to Cheerio. "That mutt isn't going to make a mess, is he?"

"Oh no, sir," I whispered. "He's taking his daily nap, which lasts until at least five this afternoon."

The doorman raised one eyebrow.

"He requires a lot of rest," I said as we made our way over to the lift. The lobby was so beautiful, it was a shame no one lived in it. Two sparkly crystal chandeliers dangled from the ceiling. Along the wall to the lift, there was a mural of people picnicking and dancing in the woods. One of the dancing women was mostly naked, but we were in such a hurry, I didn't even have time to check her out. The lift was waiting for us and I bolted for it. Ashley and Frankie were right behind me. I pushed 4 and then I noticed we were missing someone.

"Where's Robert?" I said.

Frankie stuck his head out and looked for Robert. There he was, standing in front of the mural, staring at the mostly naked lady.

"Robert! Unpeel your eyeballs and get in here," Frankie said.

Robert turned bright red. "Uh ... I was just admiring the artwork," he said.

"Right, and my name is Bernice," Frankie answered.

"I just realized something," Frankie said as we rode up. "I forgot my cape."

"No problem," I said, trying to stay calm. "We'll use your coat."

"No way, Zip. It'll stink of salami and every dog in the neighbourhood will chase me around for months."

"OK," I said. "We'll figure something else out."

"That's what I like. We'll go with the flow." Frankie rubbed his hands together and looked me right in the eye. "So what's the plan, man?"

"First," I said, "we'll get to the fourth floor."

"Yeah?"

"Then we'll get out of the lift."

"Yeah?"

"Then we'll ring the doorbell."

"Good thinking. And then?"

"And then..." I stopped and looked at Frankie. He was waiting with great expectation on his face.

"And then I don't have the slightest idea," I said.

CHAPTER 18

The lift doors opened and we got out. There was only one flat on the whole floor. I had heard that in some fancy buildings in New York, the flats are so big that they take up the whole floor of the building. I think it would be cool to live in a place like that. You could skateboard or scooter or Rollerblade up and down the hall and not disturb anyone.

The door to Flat 4B was down at the end of the hall. I glanced at Frankie, Ashley and Robert. They were expecting me to be a leader. I wasn't going to disappoint them. I shifted Cheerio in my arms and rang the bell, hoping they didn't notice that my finger was shaking all the way to the buzzer.

A tall man in a blue suit answered the door. I don't want to say he was the meanest man I've ever seen, but let's just say he didn't look happy to see us.

"You must be Mr Gristediano," I said, trying to give him my biggest smile. "I'm Hank Zipzer. Happy to meet you, sir."

I put my hand out in the basic handshake position. Papa Pete says you should always introduce yourself with a hearty handshake. It lets people know you're sincere.

"*Shhh*," the man said, putting his finger to his lips.

"Of course," I whispered. "Mr Gristediano, this is very important."

"Mr Gristediano's over there," the man in the blue suit said. "Can't you see he's conducting an important meeting?"

I stood on my tiptoes and got a peek into the living room. A group of seven or eight people, men and women in fancy suits, were sitting around on big purple sofas. The only man not wearing a tie was standing in front of a long table, on top of which sat my mum's platters. He was holding a cracker with a slice of soy salami on it and he looked like he was about to put it in his mouth. I had to stop him!

"I have to get in there," I blurted out.

Mr Blue Suit put his finger to his lips.

"You don't understand," I insisted. "I've got to stop Mr Gristediano from eating that salami."

"I'm going to have to ask you to leave," he whispered harshly.

"But that salami he's about to eat, it's got my school report in it. Also, a letter from my teacher and a manila envelope. A *large* manila envelope."

Mr Blue Suit looked at me like I was a number one nutcase and started to close the door in my face. Suddenly, Cheerio woke up. I looked down at him, and he had a look on his face I had never seen before. I could have sworn he was smiling. His nose started to twitch, and his eyes locked on something in the living room.

I followed his gaze to see what had caught his attention. There, sitting in the middle of the rug, listening to Mr Gristediano, was the largest dog I have ever seen. I think it was a Great Dane. You could have stacked up thirty-five Cheerios and still not have reached its head.

In a split second, Cheerio had jumped out of my arms and had made a beeline for that mountain of a dog, which could have easily eaten him for a snack.

"Cheerio!" I yelled. "No!"

Mr Gristediano stopped talking and turned to look at us. I didn't know what else to do. I waved. My friends were faster at thinking than I was.

Ashley pointed to Mr Blue Suit's shoes.

"Sir," she said, "your shoe's untied."

As he looked down, the four of us darted around him and ran inside. That Ashley, she has a great mind, even in a crisis.

Cheerio had reached the huge dog and was standing nose to nose with her. Cheerio sniffed her. The Great Dane sniffed back. Her sniff was so powerful that it was like a vacuum cleaner that almost lifted Cheerio's front paws off the ground. Cheerio didn't growl like he usually would have. In fact, it looked like was still smiling.

Could it be? Cheerio was falling in love!

Mr Gristediano stared at us. "Who are you, and what exactly do you think you're doing?" he demanded. The other people in the room whispered to one another. I couldn't make out their exact words, but I was pretty sure they weren't saying how great it was that we'd popped in for a visit.

"Mr Gristediano," I answered, "I can't tell you how happy we are to be here. What a nice place you have."

I had never seen such a fancy flat. Every space was filled with beautiful objects – African sculptures, china lamps, crystal candlesticks and even a pink marble chess set.

"You haven't answered my question," Mr Gristediano said. *"WHO ... ARE ... YOU?"*

"Here's the truth, Mr Gristediano, sir," I said. "It all started yesterday afternoon at about three-twenty or maybe it was three-twenty-five, when I came into my mum's deli with my report..."

Before I had a chance to finish the sentence, I heard a sound coming from Cheerio's throat. It was the weirdest sound he'd ever made, something between a purr and a howling love song.

"I don't like the sound of that, Zip," Frankie

whispered. "Your dog's going off the deep end."

Frankie has known Cheerio since he was a puppy, and he knows that when Cheerio gets started on his spinning thing, there's no stopping him.

Sure enough, Cheerio started to spin. Usually, he chases his tail because he's upset or stressed. I'd never seen him spin happily. He started to spin around so fast that you couldn't tell his head from his tail. I think he was doing it to impress the Great Dane. It worked, because before you knew it, Mr Gristediano's dog got up and started to spin too. She followed Cheerio all around the living room – to the grand piano, around the potted plants, along the front of the fireplace – like two spinning tops completely out of control.

"Nina! Down, girl!" Mr Gristediano commanded.

"Hank," said Ashley, "I think Cheerio has a crush on Nina."

"He should pick on someone his own size," said Frankie. But it was too late for that. Cheerio and Nina were spinning around a mile a minute in what I guess was some kind of weird doggie cha-cha. I'm telling you, those dogs were twirling all across the flat like two crazed ballerinas. Now, when Cheerio spins, it can

303

get pretty messy. He's been known to get our rugs twisted up in a bunch or maybe knock over an occasional lamp. But a Great Dane spinning faster than the speed of sound is a whole other thing. Nina was like a tornado travelling across the floor.

"Stop it, Nina! Stop it now!" Mr Gristediano yelled.

He grabbed her collar. Nina escaped his reach and followed Cheerio, who had twirled himself under the coffee table. Nina tried to get under there too, but she couldn't fit, so she spun around next to it. *SWISH!* Her tail whipped around and landed smack on the pink chess set. The pieces shot into the air like missiles, and all the well-dressed people sitting on the sofa scattered so they wouldn't get hit by a flying bishop or a knight on horseback.

"What on earth is going on?" asked a woman with short black hair.

"Take cover!" shouted a chubby man with a bow tie. He crawled behind the sofa, but he wasn't fast enough to avoid getting smacked in the behind by a flying rook. Luckily, his behind was well padded, and the chess piece just bounced off and fell on to the carpet.

One of the pawns landed on Cheerio's tail, and he let out a little yip. He bolted from under the coffee table and spun himself over towards the picture window that looked out at the Hudson River.

"Cheerio!" I yelled. "Come! Or if not come, then stop!"

Nina went galumphing after Cheerio, who was now dangerously close to one of the African sculptures. It was a sculpture of a man holding a baby up to the sky.

"Oh no," Frankie said.

But *oh yes*. Nina's tail thrashed into the wooden sculpture. The sculpture toppled, like a quarterback being tackled. It landed on the floor with a thud. A few of the guests gasped, but one man, who I recognized as the manager of our local Gristediano's, actually chuckled a little.

"Clean up on aisle five," he said, giving the woman next to him a nudge. The woman next to him didn't even laugh a little.

Mr Blue Suit ran to the sculpture and tried to stand it up again.

"Here, let me help you," I said.

"Stay away, whoever you are!" he yelled. "You've done all the damage you're going to do!"

That's what he thought.

By now, Cheerio and Nina were doing their dance across the centre of the room, taking down everything in their path. *Bam* went a vase with blue flowers all over it. *Rip* went the pillows on the fancy purple sofa. Smash went the carved crystal candlesticks. *Bam! Pow! Crunch!* went the three china ducks on the end table. Boy, if I had ever seen *break*-dancing, this was it.

Cheerio was having the time of his life. If he had cheeks and they weren't furry, they would have been glowing. Nina was having quite a fun time herself. She didn't seem to care that Mr Gristediano was shouting every command he knew.

"Stay! Lie Down! Sit! Come! Heel! Up! Down! Off!" he screamed.

Nothing was working. All the people in their business suits were crouched in the corners of the room and behind the sofa. Mr Gristediano was running after Nina, and I was running after Cheerio. Those two lovesick dogs couldn't have cared less about us. They totally ignored us, spinning their way to the centre of the room near the table of my mum's cold cuts. The vibrations made the platters rattle and shake. One of the platters had shifted to the edge of the table and was about to fall. I pushed it back and grabbed a slice of soy salami from it. I held it up.

"Here, Cheerio!" I said. "A treat!"

I thought if I got his attention, he'd stop spinning for a minute and then I could grab him. Instead, I got Nina's attention, which was not my plan.

Nina jumped up to get the salami, and as she came down, her giant tail swept across the table, knocking all the platters into the air. There were trays of meat sailing around like Frisbees. Slices

of soy salami flew everywhere, scattering like fireworks on Bonfire night. Nina was grabbing them out of the air. She got them before they even hit the ground, ate some of them and gave a few to Cheerio, since jumping isn't exactly his strong point.

I looked at some of the salami that had landed on the rug. I think I saw the word *sloppy* in one and the word *fail* in another. I know I saw *Ms Adolf* in another one – the words, not actually her.

Cheerio must have got one with a big chunk of something in it, because he was having a tough time chewing up his slice. I looked down at him. He held the salami between his front paws, trying like crazy to gnaw through a chunk of manila folder that was wadded up in it. He was so busy concentrating that he was standing still for the first time since he crashed the party.

"Let's get him," I said to the others.

Frankie, Ashley, Robert and I joined hands and made a tight circle. We crept up on him, and before he could say "arf", we had him surrounded. I scooped him up and held him tight in my arms.

Poor Cheerio. Love was hard on him. He was

exhausted. His little heart was racing and he was panting. His tongue was hanging out of his mouth and it still had a piece of soy salami clinging to it. I lifted the salami out of his mouth so he wouldn't choke on it. When I looked at it, I couldn't believe my eyes. There, lying in the salami for all to see, was my *D* in spelling.

That rotten mark was going to follow me wherever I went.

CHAPTER 19

We're friends, right? So you know me by now – at least a little bit. So you've probably figured out that when bad things happen to me, I make lists in my head.

That's exactly what I did as I looked around the mess that used to be Mr Gristediano's beautiful flat.

THE NEXT SIX THINGS I PREDICT
WILL HAPPEN TO ME

BY HANK ZIPZER

(ALSO KNOWN AS
"CAPTAIN DESTRUCTO")

1. Mr Gristediano, who is really a genie in
   disguise, will grant me three wishes.
   For my first wish, I will wish that none of
   this ever happened, and it won't have.
2. For my second wish, I will wish for front-row
   season tickets to the Mets' games.
   I will get them.
3. While sitting in my box at the Mets game,
   I will catch more foul balls than any fan
   ever has.
4. They will offer me a position on the Mets
   as centre fielder. I will accept the position
   and become the youngest baseball player
   in America.
5. For my third wish, I will wish for world
   peace, because that's what Papa Pete
   always wishes for when he blows out
   his birthday candles.
6. I will become world famous as a peace
   loving baseball star.

CHAPTER 20

You must have guessed by now that Numbers 1 to 6 didn't come true.

Instead, what happened was that Mr Gristediano called my parents and said that he had to see them right away about a very serious matter.

So much for my predictions. I guess I don't have much of a future in the crystal ball business.

CHAPTER 21

The hardest thing in the world is waiting, especially when you're waiting for bad news. It only took twenty minutes for my parents to get to Mr Gristediano's, but it seemed like twenty years.

I asked Papa Pete if he would take Ashley, Frankie and Robert home. They got into this mess to help me out. I didn't see any reason for them to have to be there to take the blame. Papa Pete told me he was proud of that decision, because I was taking responsibility for my own actions. Before he left, he took my face in his hands and whispered, "Remember, Hankie: *truth*. That's the magic word."

Papa Pete took Cheerio home too. Poor Cheerio. After Mr Gristediano's store managers had left, Cheerio had flopped down next to the fireplace and started to lick the bricks as though they were doggie treats. Don't ask me why. You just can't explain a lot of what Cheerio does. Nina wanted to play with him, but Cheerio had lost all interest in her. That's him. In love one minute, licking bricks the next.

When we were alone, I offered to help Mr Gristediano clean up the mess in his flat.

"I think you've done enough damage already," he said. He was holding the pieces of one of the china ducks that had broken in half.

"I bought these ducks in Italy," he said. "I paid a pretty penny for them, as I recall."

"I'm really sorry, Mr Gristediano," I said. "I didn't mean to break anything."

He didn't answer. I couldn't blame him. I'd be angry at me too, if I were him.

I bent down and started to pick up the chess pieces that were scattered all across the floor. I had to do something to help. Very carefully, I put them back on the board the way they were supposed to go.

"I see you play chess," Mr Gristediano said.

"My grandpa taught me."

He began to sweep up the pieces of the blue-flowered vase. It was quiet.

"Do you play chess?" I asked.

"Yes," he said. "My father taught me. He played a lot of chess."

"My dad does crossword puzzles," I said.

"Do you do them too?"

"No way. I'm a terrible speller."

"Me too," he said. "I was a teenager before I could spell my name correctly."

"Really?"

"Really. Of course, it's not that easy when your name is Vincenzo Giovanni Giuseppe Gristediano. My brother got off easy. His name is Mike."

I laughed. Mr Gristediano smiled for the first time since the disaster. I couldn't believe he could smile after all the trouble I had caused.

The doorman downstairs rang the buzzer to say my parents had arrived. I sighed. And there it was – the moment I definitely had not been waiting for.

When my mum came in and saw the mess, she shot me one of her mum looks. It was the one that says, "I don't know what you've done, but how could you have done it?" You've probably received that look sometime in your life. My dad had a different look on his face. It was the same one he had the time he went to the dentist for a root canal on his back molar.

"Let me just say that we are so sorry," my mum began.

"Of course, we'll take care of everything that's broken," my dad added.

Mr Gristediano offered them a seat on the sofa. My dad sat down, then reached under his bum and pulled out a piece of salami that had got wedged in between the pillows. When he put the salami into the ashtray on the coffee table, I could see a wad of manila envelope mashed up inside it.

"Hank, I think you need to tell your parents what happened here today," Mr Gristediano said. "I'm sure they would like an explanation, as would I."

Listen, I can make up a story at the drop of a hat, right?

Sitting there on the sofa with all of them waiting for me to talk, I was tempted. I could have said that alien worms invaded the salami and planted secret papers in it. I could have said that a superhero named Captain Destructo told me to destroy all lunch meats to save the world from the evils of soy.

Truth, I heard Papa Pete say in my mind's ear.

And so I told the truth, the whole truth and nothing but the truth.

I started at the very beginning, with the three *D*s on my school report. I told them how ashamed I was of those marks. I described everything that happened after that – the meat grinder, the recipe switch, the plan to seize the salami. At the end, I even pointed out the chunk of brown manila folder wadded up in the salami on the coffee table.

My parents could not believe what they were hearing. Their mouths were hanging open so wide that you could have planted trees in there.

There are no words to describe how they reacted. Well, maybe there are. *Angry. Embarrassed. Shocked. Disappointed. Hot under the collar.* (Sorry, that's three words. Oops, I mean four.) If I knew how to spell *infuriated*, I'd put that down too.

I'm out of words now, so let me just say this: imagine confessing to your mum or dad the worst thing you've ever done. Imagine what their faces would look like. Imagine how their voices would sound. Imagine steam coming out of the top of their heads. You get the picture? Good, because that's just how my parents looked when I finished talking.

"Hank, how could you?" my mum asked. She turned to Mr Gristediano. "We don't know what Hank was thinking."

"You'd better get used to your room," my dad said to me, "because you'll be spending all your time there."

"I don't want to butt in to your family business," Mr Gristediano said, "but may I make a suggestion?"

I was sure he was going to suggest that I go to jail and just eat bread and water.

"This sounds like a situation I had in my own family," Mr Gristediano said. "With my middle daughter, Angela."

"She ground her school report up into lunch meat too?" I asked.

"I'm sure she would have liked to," Mr Gristediano said. "Angela was a very bright child who did very poorly at school. We were always so frustrated with her, and even worse, she was always frustrated with herself. She grew to believe she just wasn't clever."

Boy, do I know how she felt, I thought.

"When she got to junior high school, one of Angela's teachers suggested that we get her tested to see if she had any learning difficulties. It turned out she did. Angela was clever, don't get me wrong. She just learned differently to how a lot of other kids do. Do you know that one out of every five kids has learning difficulties? I'm sure I had them too, but when I was growing up, no one even knew there was such a thing."

Mr Gristediano had trouble learning? No way. He owned the biggest supermarket chain in all of New York.

"Where is Angela now?" my mum asked.

"She's a senior at Columbia University," said Mr Gristediano. "Once we figured out how she learned best, we got her help and her marks improved dramatically. In fact, everything changed for her."

"I assume you're telling us this for a reason," my dad said.

"As I listened to Hank just now, he reminded me so much of my Angela, and of myself too," Mr Gristediano said. "His frustration. His shame in failing. It's all so unnecessary. I'm no expert, but if Hank were my son, I'd see about getting him tested."

I looked over at my mum and dad. We all said the same thing at the same time: "Mr Rock."

That's exactly what Mr Rock had said after I'd spent that week in detention with him. He said he thought I should be tested to see if I have learning difficulties. He even came over to our house to tell my parents that. He said exactly what Mr Gristediano had just said, but without the Angela part.

When Mr Rock suggested it, my mum thought it was a good idea to get me tested, but my dad refused. Instead, he gave me a lecture about his Stanley Zipzer theory of success in school. According to his theory, all you have to do is "put your butt in your chair and study" and you'll do fine. End of story.

I've never been able to convince my dad that I really do study. I study; I just don't learn.

That's not exactly true. I learn some things. In fact, a lot of things are really easy for me – like memorizing poems or remembering facts from history. My brain just gobbles up that stuff like Hershey's Kisses. But other subjects, like spelling or maths or drawing – those are really hard. I feel as though when I try to learn those things, my brain says, "Sorry, I'm closed."

Before we left, my parents again offered to pay Mr Gristediano for everything that Cheerio had destroyed.

"I'll tell you what," he said. "You can pay me back by looking into the testing."

My dad didn't say anything, but my mum said she would make arrangements right away.

As we left, I apologized to Mr Gristediano for causing so much trouble.

"I hope you learned something from everything that happened today," he said. "Growing up is tough, Hank. It's not all smooth sailing." Boy, was he nice.

We were pretty quiet the whole walk home. When we got back to our apartment, my mum went right into her bedroom.

I could hear her dialling on the phone.

CHAPTER 22

The testing place looked just like an office at school, which isn't surprising because it *was* an office at school. The walls were covered with lots of posters that kids had drawn. One showed a colourful butterfly. Another showed a family of puppies in a basket telling whoever was looking at them to read a lot. Those puppies were cute enough to play with.

The tester was Dr Lynn Berger. She smiled when she talked and kept telling me to take deep breaths and relax. She must have been hanging out with Frankie.

We sat at a round table facing each other. Dr Berger had a little table right next to her with all her equipment on it: blocks, Lego, pictures, pencils and lots of paper. I mean *lots* of it. Some pages were blank, some had shapes and some were divided into four squares.

I was nervous. I wasn't sure why. Maybe because I hate taking tests or maybe because I was worried the tests would tell everyone that I was stupid for real.

"Well, shall we begin?" Dr Berger asked.

"Sure," I answered, not really meaning it.

"OK. First, I'm going to put a piece of paper in front of you and ask you to draw your family – pets and all."

"Does neatness count?" I asked.

"No, Hank. This is not about you being an artist," Dr Berger assured me.

I picked up the pencil and stared at the blank piece of white paper for a while. I didn't know how to draw people without making them look like sticks.

"Can I go and get a drink of water?" I asked.

Dr Berger went to the corner of the room, where there was a water cooler. She pushed the blue button and water rushed out into a paper

324

cup. She handed me the cup. I took a small sip. I wasn't really thirsty; I had just wanted to get out of there.

"Try to relax, Hank. You're fine," she said.

I drew a little squiggle on the paper. It looked like a hair.

"Do you understand what I asked for?" Dr Berger asked. "I want you to draw any kind of picture of your family."

"I understand. I'm sorry," I said. I wasn't exactly positive why I was apologizing, but it sounded right.

I started with Stan the crossword-puzzle man. I tried drawing him sitting at the dining room table doing a crossword puzzle. The table got so big that it took up almost the whole page, so I put the rest of the family there too. Everyone in the family was on one side of the table, facing me. Mum, Dad and Emily, with Katherine on her shoulder. I even put a little piece of iguana poo on Emily's sweater. Cheerio was under the table. He came out looking like one of those really long bubbles that I used to blow when I was little.

"I hope this is right," I said to Dr Berger.

"There are no right or wrong answers on this test," she said.

"I wish all my tests were like that," I said to her.

Dr Berger laughed, and I started to relax a little bit.

I sat back and looked at my picture. I noticed that we all looked exactly alike – even the iguana. Now I started laughing, because it struck me as funny that Mum had three twins and one of them was a green reptile with a mile-long tongue.

Dr Berger asked me what was so amusing.

"It's just that my sister's pet iguana looks like her twin," I said.

"Do you all have dinner together?"

"Yes. Every night."

"My, such a lovely family you have."

"That's easy for you to say, because you haven't seen my dad in his boxer shorts."

Wherever that thought came from, please let it go back there right away!

Dr Berger laughed again. What a great audience.

The next part of the test involved putting a set

of odd-shaped blocks into exactly the same pattern as the one drawn on a sheet of paper. Dr Berger put the blocks in front of me.

I pushed them around until I lined them up perfectly to look just like the pattern on the test paper.

"Wow! You accomplished that task in record time!" Dr Berger said.

"No kidding. Was I the fastest person ever?"

"I'm sure you are one of them," she said.

That felt good. I began to think that maybe this testing thing was going to work out just fine.

There was reading and vocabulary and listening to numbers and having to repeat them back. I worked on puzzles, looked at splattered paintings and arranged pictures in order. Some of the activities were fun, which made the time really speed by.

When we were all done, Dr Berger walked me out to the hall, where my parents were waiting. She told us she would go over the results and we would hear back in about a week. Hear what? Hear that I had to change schools? Be left behind? That I'm not clever enough to go to school in the first place?

Boy, seven days can be an awfully long time.

CHAPTER 23

When I'm nervous, my body turns into a fountain. If I'm a little bit nervous, my forehead gets damp. If I'm medium nervous, my palms start to sweat. If I'm really nervous, the armpits get involved. And when I'm scared, my back actually sweats. That may be too much information for you, but there it is, I've said it.

As I sat outside Head Teacher Love's office, all of the above were happening at once. Sweat was trickling out of every part of me that could trickle.

They had been inside there for half an hour – Mr Love, Dr Berger, and my mum and dad. They'd said that they wanted to review my test results in private before they called me in. I knew if my tests had turned out normal, my parents would have been out of there in two minutes. I mean, how long does it take to say, "Great kid you got there"? Not half an hour, I can tell you that.

Mr Rock had seen me waiting in the hall. He said he was really glad my parents had agreed to get me tested and he thought life at PS 87 was going to be much better for me now. Before he left, he handed me a packet of tissues and said I could keep them to mop myself up. It was nice of him not to mention that I was sweating like a hog. After I used the tissues to dry my face, I screwed each one up into a ball and shot them into the bin with my foot. I made seven out of seven, so sitting in the hallway wasn't a total loss.

Frankie came running down the stairs, two at a time.

"How'd you get out of class?" I asked him.

"I volunteered to take the register to the office," he said. "Any news from Mole Man?"

"Not yet. I'm pretty nervous."

"Release the tension, Zip," he suggested. "Let

it flow up your spine and out of your third eye."
The third eye is a yoga term for some place on your
body. I have no idea where, but I keep looking for it.

"What kind of freak has three eyes?" asked a
big, nasty voice from behind us. That could only be
one person. It was Nick McKelty, the last person
you want to see when you're waiting to find out if
you're normal or not.

"How's the boy genius?" Nick the Tick asked,
pointing towards me. "They figure out what's
wrong with you yet?"

Frankie waved his hands around in the air.

"*Zengawii!*" he said. "That means disappear, McKelty."

"Ms Adolf sent me to find *you*," Nick said to Frankie. "She thought you'd got lost."

"Why would she send *you*?" answered Frankie. "You couldn't find your way out of a paper bag."

"Oh yeah?" asked McKelty. He scratched his huge blond head, trying to think of a comeback. "Oh yeah?" he asked again. Then he turned and left. He's a quick one, that McKelty.

The door opened and Dr Berger stepped out.

"Hank, we're ready for you now," she said.

"They're going to tell me I'm stupid," I whispered to Frankie.

"Right, and my name is Bernice," he whispered back.

I took a deep breath and walked into the office.

My mum was holding a yellow pad with her notes on it. My dad had a report in a blue cover. My name was printed on the outside. It was thick – probably twenty pages long. Wow, someone had a lot to say about me.

"We've had a nice chat with your parents," Dr

Berger began. "I want to begin by telling you how much I appreciated your co-operation during the testing process, Hank. You gave it your best effort, and I'm proud of you for that."

This wasn't sounding good at all. I've played enough football to know that when the coach talks about a good effort, he's usually talking to the losing team.

"We've gone over your test results," Dr Berger went on. "You have exceptional verbal and reasoning skills, an outstanding vocabulary, great creativity and a superior intelligence."

"You mean I'm clever?" I asked. I felt all the tension going up my spine and out of my third eye.

"Yes, Hank, you are. But along with that..."

No, I thought. *Don't say anything more. Just stop right there.*

"The tests also show that you have some learning difficulties that have been getting in the way of your school performance," she said.

Well, there it was. I have learning difficulties. The truth was out.

I didn't know what to think.

"So what you're saying is that I'm clever and stupid at the same time," I said.

"Absolutely not. You're not stupid at all, Hank," Dr Berger answered. "Everybody learns in different ways. Our job is to find the best way for you to learn. And I think we can do that."

"How?"

"Oh, there are lots of ways," she said. "We're going to start by working on your study skills so we can help you focus better."

OK. That didn't sound too bad.

"Sometimes I learn something and then forget it all overnight," I said. "Is that because I don't focus?"

"Perhaps," she said. "We're also going to talk to your teacher about letting you get information in different ways, like listening to tapes, for example."

I like tapes. This was actually sounding pretty good.

"Listening and watching," I said. "I can do that."

"Good," she answered. "And we'll give you all the time you need to take your tests."

Extra time on tests? Man, I felt like I wanted to jump out of my chair and give Dr Berger a big kiss on the cheek.

Wait a minute. As I thought more about that, I wasn't sure how I felt about it. I mean, Frankie and Ashley would be finished and at home having dinner and I'd still be at school, taking a test.

I noticed that my parents had been very quiet during all this.

"Are you mad at me?" I asked them.

"For what?" my mum asked.

"For having learning differences."

My mum reached out and took my hand.

"Of course not, honey. We're going to help you every way we can."

"Good," I said. "How about two real chocolate puddings – not low fat – every night for dessert. I think that would help me a lot."

"Same old Hank," my father said. He sounded grumpy, but he was actually smiling.

"We'll all be keeping close watch on your progress," said Mr Love.

Uh-oh. That sounded to me like I was going to be putting in extra mole time with Mr Love and the

Statue of Liberty there on his face.

"Does that mean I'll be coming to see you more often?" I asked. "Not that I don't enjoy our visits, of course."

"I hope that as your school work improves, we'll see an improvement in your behaviour," said Mr Love.

I noticed that I had stopped sweating.

"If you have questions about any of this, don't be afraid to ask," said Dr Berger. She stood up.

I put out my hand, in the basic handshake position Papa Pete had taught me. She took my hand and shook it.

"Thank you," I said to Dr Berger. "Thank you for everything."

And you know what? I meant it.

CHAPTER 24

That night we made a homework chart and taped it on the bedroom wall over my desk. On one side, we wrote the name of every subject I study at school. Next to each subject, we made boxes for every night of the week. When I finished my homework in each subject, I would get a sticker in the box.

"That's not fair," said Emily. "I want stickers, too."

The next night, Papa Pete came over with a surprise. He brought two big rolls of stickers. The ones with the snakes on them were for Emily. The ones with the Mets baseballs and Shea Stadium were mine.

"You're going to make it to the World Series of homework," Papa Pete said.

Papa Pete and I went outside on the balcony and sat down. It was cold, but we felt warm with our big coats on. Papa Pete took out a plastic bag from his pocket. He took out two pickles, our favourite snack. He handed me a garlic dill and took the other one for himself. They were so juicy that they squirted when we bit into them.

"Hankie, let me know if I get any seeds in the old handlebars," he said.

I looked at his moustache. "You're all clear, Papa Pete."

We sat there for a minute, crunching on our pickles and enjoying the air.

"Look at that moon," he said.

If you crane your neck and look around the corner of our balcony, sometimes you can see the moon.

"It's so round. Guess what it reminds me of?" Papa Pete asked.

When most grown-ups ask you to guess at something, they don't really want you to. Papa Pete does.

"Give me a clue," I said.

"It's something you eat."

"A ball of cheddar cheese."

He shook his head no.

"Give me another clue."

"Something your mother makes."

"A matzo ball."

He shook his head no.

"One more clue," I begged.

"Something your mother specializes in."

"A slice of soy salami."

"Bingo," he said.

I was quiet. I still felt really terrible about ruining my mum's chances at that big order for Mr Gristediano. I hadn't been able to say the words *soy salami* since.

"I really messed up her chances, didn't I?" I asked. "And she was so excited about it too."

"The good thing about mistakes," said Papa Pete, "is that sometimes we have a chance to make them right."

"I can't fix what I did," I said. "There's no way."

Papa Pete didn't answer. He just sat there and

finished his pickle. Then he got to his feet.

"If you were to think of some way," he said, "I happen to be free tomorrow afternoon. You're a smart boy. Think it over."

I thought in the shower. I thought while I was putting on my pyjamas. I thought while I was brushing my teeth. By the time I had put my head on the pillow, I was done thinking. I had thought of a plan.

CHAPTER 25

Papa Pete met me after school.

"Where to?" he asked.

"The ninety-nine-cent shop," I answered.

The ninety-nine-cent shop is on Amsterdam Avenue, right under McKelty's Roll 'N Bowl. I do a lot of my gift shopping there, because ninety-nine cents is just the right price range for my gift budget.

We walked inside and I went up to the woman at the till.

"Excuse me, do you have chess sets?" I said.

"Aisle thirty-seven," she answered.

You don't get much in the way of a chess set for ninety-nine cents. There were only two choices: a flimsy cardboard one with plastic pieces or a small one that was made for travelling. I liked the small one. It looked like it was made in China, because the faces on the pieces were dragons. I bought the chess set and a silver bow to put on top.

"Where to now?" asked Papa Pete.

"Follow me," I said.

We walked to Riverside Drive. When we reached number 451, the doorman with the shiny gold buttons on his coat came outside.

"Well, look who's back," he said. "The boy with the exploding salamis." He had a good laugh to himself. I couldn't blame him, really.

"Would you please ask Mr Gristediano if I can come up?" I asked.

"I'll warn him," the doorman said, "so he can put away anything valuable." He laughed again. "Hey, I'm just kidding with ya."

I invited Papa Pete up, but he said that he'd wait downstairs in the park. I walked through the lobby, past the mostly naked lady on the wall. Why was it that both times I'd been there, I hadn't had time to stop and admire the artwork, as Robert would say? It wasn't fair.

Mr Gristediano and Nina were waiting for me at the door. Nina sniffed my clothes. She must have smelled Cheerio, because her tail started to wag like crazy.

"This is for you," I said to Mr Gristediano, handing him the chess set with the silver bow. "I picked it out myself. It's not much, but I wanted to say thank you for suggesting that I get tested."

"How did that go?" he asked.

"It turns out I do have some learning difficulties," I said. I hadn't told anyone that before, but I figured it was time to start. "The woman who tested me says we're going to work on them."

"Good for you," said Mr Gristediano. "It takes a brave man to be honest with himself."

He looked at the box in his hand. "Should I open this?"

I nodded.

"Why, this is a perfect gift, Hank," he said. "You know how much I like chess. Would you like to come in for a game?"

I was hoping he'd ask.

We sat down at the table by the picture window. I set up the board and we started to play. It was a nice place for a chess game. When it wasn't your turn, you could look out of the window and watch the boats going up and down the Hudson River.

"I missed lunch today," I said to Mr Gristediano. "Do you mind if I have a little snack?"

I reached into my rucksack and got out the sandwich my mum had made for lunch. I don't think I have to tell you what kind it was. I took a bite.

"What kind of sandwich is it?" Mr Gristediano asked.

I lifted up the top piece of bread and showed him. "It's soy salami," I said.

I took another bite.

"Mr Gristediano, do you want to try this? It just might make your taste buds stand up and salute. I can't honestly say it has that effect on me, but it does for a lot of people."

Mr Gristediano laughed, and I silently thanked Papa Pete for teaching me that expression.

"You're making it sound awfully tempting," he said.

I took the other half of the sandwich and handed it to Mr Gristediano. He took a bite.

"It's really good for you," I said. "No preservatives, no artificial colours. I've heard soy salami called the lunch meat of the twenty-first century."

"This is quite good," said Mr Gristediano. "It wouldn't happen to be from your mother's deli, would it?"

"You mean The Crunchy Pickle at Seventy-seventh and Broadway?" I asked. "The one that's open until six tonight? Why, yes, it is."

I moved my queen across the board.

"By the way, I believe that's checkmate," I said.

I had caught Mr Gristediano by surprise.

"You're a smart boy, Hank," he said. "I like you."

"Thank you," I said.

He took the last bite of his half of the sandwich.

"And I like your mother's soy salami too."

CHAPTER 26

"**Guess who came into the deli today!**" my mum said as she rushed into our flat that night.

"King Kong," said Emily. She and Papa Pete were reading a pop-up book on gorillas.

"Mr Gristediano!" Mum said. She took off her hat, threw it up in the air and let out a scream. "He just walked in and said he wanted to place an order."

"How big an order?" my dad asked, looking up from his crossword puzzle.

"One hundred cases!" Mum said.

"That's one thousand nine hundred and twenty salamis!" my father said. He jumped out of his chair, grabbed my mum and spun her around the room.

Papa Pete flashed me the kind of grin that said we knew something they didn't know.

"Mr Gristediano said that any woman who can invent the lunch meat of the twenty-first century and raise a fine son like Hank Zipzer deserves to get a great big order!"

"He said that?" I asked.

"Word for word," my mum said. "We have you to thank for this, Hank." She was so happy that she was crying.

My mum gave me such a huge hug that I couldn't catch my breath. Then our whole family started to hug. My dad hugged Emily. Papa Pete hugged my mum. My dad hugged me. Emily hugged Katherine. Cheerio tried to hug himself. I hugged Emily ... but just for a second. We went hugging crazy, there's no doubt about it.

"Here's to Hank," Papa Pete said.

"Here's to Hank," everyone repeated.

I took a bow.

"You should be very proud of yourself, son," my dad said.

"Me?" I asked. "What'd I do, Dad?"

"You've brought your marks up – way up."

"I did?"

"Just a few days ago, you had a *D* in salami," he said. "And now look. I'm giving you an *A* in salami!"

I threw my arms around my dad and laughed. It was the first *A* my father had given me. Hey, it was my first *A* ever. And it sure felt good.

An interview with Henry Winkler

What's your favourite thing about Hank Zipzer?

My favourite thing about Hank Zipzer is that he is resourceful. Just because he can't figure something out doesn't mean that he won't find a way. I love his sense of humour. Even though Lin and I write the books together, when we meet in the morning to work we never know where the characters or the story will take us. Hank and his friends make us laugh all the time.

Hank likes to write lists. Are you a list person, too? (If so, what sorts of lists do you make?)

Hank likes to write lists, and so do I. My whole life is organized on scraps of paper in a pile on my desk by my phone. If I didn't make lists, I would get nothing done, because I would forget the important things that I had to do. And then, I'm constantly rewriting those lists and adding to them. So yes, I'm a list maker.

Who was your favourite teacher?

Believe it or not, Mr Rock, the music teacher at my high school, McBurney's School for Boys, was my favourite teacher. He seemed to understand that learning was difficult for me. He understood that just because I had trouble with almost every subject, it did not mean I was stupid.

Where did you grow up?

I grew up on the West side of New York City in the same building Hank lives in. The neighbourhood, the stores, the park, the school and even Ms Adolf are all taken from my life. I took the Broadway bus number 104 to school every day.

What was it like growing up with dyslexia?

When I was growing up in New York City, no one knew what dyslexia was. I was called stupid and lazy, and I was told that I was not living up to my potential. It was, without a doubt, painful. I spent most of my time covering up the fact that reading, writing, spelling, maths, science – actually, every subject but lunch – was really, really difficult for me. If I went to the shop and paid the bill with paper money and I was given coins back for change, I had no idea how to count up the change in my head. I just trusted that everyone was being honest.

What's it like working as a team to write the World's Greatest Underachiever books?

We have the most wonderful time working together. Lin sits at the computer, and I walk in a circle in front of her desk. If I start talking like the characters, Lin kindly types it in because I don't use a computer. Or, she'll tell me to stop for minute because she's got a great idea and her fingers fly across the keyboard. Sometimes, I'll write my chapters in long hand and Lin will transcribe them and correct my spelling. When the book is done, we both go over it to see if we've left anything out, or perhaps we'll find a better joke for one of the characters or better action in a scene. When it's completely done, we send it to our editor, and she sends back her notes that we then incorporate.

Did you always want to be an author?

Until the day that I met Lin Oliver for lunch in 2002, I never thought about being an author for one minute in my whole life.

How long does it take you to write a book?

It usually takes about two months to write the first draft of a book. Lin and I meet in her office and create the outline for the story of the book and then, two months later, we have a 153-page adventure about Hank Zipzer.

Which of your books do you like the best?

I cannot pick one book that I like the best. Each one of them is like my own child. Each one of them has some great detail that makes me laugh every time I think about it.